Edward Hayes Plumptre

Master and Scholar

Edward Hayes Plumptre

Master and Scholar

ISBN/EAN: 9783337395742

Printed in Europe, USA, Canada, Australia, Japan

Cover: Foto ©Andreas Hilbeck / pixelio.de

More available books at **www.hansebooks.com**

MASTER AND SCHOLAR

ETC. ETC.

By E. H. PLUMPTRE, M.A.

ALEXANDER STRAHAN, PUBLISHER
LONDON AND NEW YORK
1866

TO

𝕿𝖍𝖊 𝕸𝖊𝖒𝖔𝖗𝖌

OF

JOHN KEBLE.

———

ONE star of song from out our firmament
 Hath passed away, and lo! a vacant space,
 Where once rich music flowed from lips of grace
And soothed the murmurs of our discontent:
Silent the voice that once its sweetness sent
 Through all the windings of the Christian's year,
 Or sang to lyre attuned for listening ear
Of child-like souls whose name is "Innocent."
Hush, faithless grief! This Easter morning bright
 Its witness bears nor star nor voice is gone:
That still shines clear for all who love the light;
 This through far lands and ages soundeth on;
Ah! Were it ours to tune our lives aright,
 Nor basely fail where he hath nobly won!

Easter, 1866.

CONTENTS.

TRANSLATIONS.

MASTER AND SCHOLAR.

I.

SCENE—*A Franciscan House.* St Ebbe's, Oxford.
A winter sunrise, 1267.

ROGER BACON *sitting at a desk, dressed as a Franciscan friar, barefooted.*

THE dawn is breaking, thick and gray the mists
    Float upward from the meadows, and the frost
Hangs, silver crystalled, on each feathery bough;
Slowly the river creeps through banks of ice,
Itself half frozen; and the cold clear moon
Still lingers in the west, while golden rays
Light up the spires and towers of yonder town,
Transfigured into beauty.   Others wake
From wonted slumbers.   Priests and students flock
To chant their matins, and the peasant churl
Seeks fuel in the forest; but to me
Sleep comes not yet.   I keep my vigil late,
And through the cold long night I labour still,
For, lo! the night comes on when none can work.

A

[*Writes, and then pauses.*

And so my task is ended, and I close
The labour of my life.   This worn-out pen
Has done good service.   All my search for truth,
The search through this wide-spreading universe,
The wonders of the earth and of the deep,
The glories of yon star-decked firmament,
The search within through all the maze of life,
The thoughts that come and go, the subtle law
By which men pass from ignorance to doubt,
From doubt to truth, from truth in lower things
To truth in higher, onward, onward still,
Till knowledge ends in wonder, and the soul,
Sated yet craving, stops in weariness,
And then we kneel before the throne, and veil
Our faces, like the Cherubim who stand,
Their rainbow wings enwrapping face and feet,
And evermore cry "Holy is the Lord!"—
All this has reached its end, and what I know,
The treasure God has given me from His store,
Lies here within this casket.   So my work,
This greater work than all my former toils,
Shall live throughout the ages.   Now I fade,
My strength is dwindling, and my name despised,
Cast out as evil, and the night is dark,
And I have none like-minded.   O'er my grave
But few will weep, and few will miss the face
Of him they slander.   But a time will come,

When Truth shall shine in brightness from the clouds,
And the loud din of babbling crows and choughs
Being hushed in silence, her almighty voice
Shall speak in clear low whispers, rising up
At last to trumpet loudness.   Then my name
Shall not be all forgotten.   Men will think
Of one who sowed the harvest they shall reap,
Who led the way through forests thick and dark,
Their dank, foul branches shadowing all the land,
And cleared a path for those that followed him,
O'er crag and moss advancing, undismayed
By stormiest blasts or wild lights of the fen.
So shall the years pass on as now they pass,
And boys and youths and men shall mingle still
Where Thamis flows through fields of Oxenford,
And run their race, and pass from hand to hand
The burning torch of knowledge.   Still each spring
Shall see the same bright faces flushed with hopes,
The wonder of a soul that looks on life,
As looks a traveller on a land unknown,
Fair vales and woods and towers, from snowy height
Of distant Alp ; and still youth's pride of strength
Shall overflow its bounds.   When winter binds,
As now, the waters, o'er the glassy plain
Shall glide the nimble feet, and eyes be bright
With glowing health ; and when the leaves are green,
And summer suns are hot upon the fields,
And May-flies sport their filmy wings of gold,

From bank and copse the merry laugh shall ring,
And forms well knit as when the sculptors old
Wrought young Apollo's glory, plunging in,
Where by the willows flows the deepening stream,
Shall gleam in shade or sunshine.   Strong and brave,
In them shall England find her noblest sons ;
The swift-winged oar shall bear them on the floods ;
The mimic strife of arms shall train their limbs
To deeds of knightly prowess, and the years
Of youth shall gather friends who shall not fail,
When manhood passes to the autumn sere
Of withered age.   And there, in time to come,
Shall those who travail not for meed of praise,
Or earthly honour, or the draff of swine,
Be as the priests who in the Temple wait
And do their service, choosing Wisdom fair,
In her unearthly beauty.   Slowly moves
The triumph of that Wisdom, and its wheels
Drive heavily.   The ruts which men have made,
Each for his little system, make the road
Both rough and full of danger ; but in time
It comes, and will not tarry.   We must wait
In patience its appearing.   I can die,
Rejoicing that the towers I look upon
Shall meet the eyes of thousands who shall love
Their beauty as I love them, who shall hear
Those clear-voiced bells ring out the midnight chimes,
As I have heard them.   Then the circling years

Shall lead the pilgrim forward on his way
In search of wisdom. Truths that I have known
In seed and germ shall quicken into growth,
The blade, the ear, the full corn in the ear ;
These lines and circles that I trace, in faith
My labours shall not perish, they shall be
For hands more skilled than mine, the pregnant hints
For cunning works surpassing former thoughts,
The wonder of the future. Armed with these,
Each sense shall widen. Sun and moon and stars
Shall yield their secrets. Men shall know the laws
That guide them in their courses, watch each phase
Of all their circling movement, find at last
The secret of their dread, sweet influence
On us and on our fortunes. Or, perchance,
For so my thoughts have whispered, we shall see
God's order plainly. These bewildering mists,
Haze of hot fancies, giving form and hue
To merest dreams, shall pass away, and leave
The Wisdom which we see in earth and heaven
More bright than ever. Change the subtle art,
And Man's weak eyes shall search into a world
As yet unknown, where myriad forms of life,
Swarming in bough, or dust, or lake, or stream,
The subtlest tissues of the flow'ret's crown,
That golden film that forms the May-fly's wing,
The wondrous transformations of the force
That circles through all being, these shall ope

Their secret stores, and Nature, like the king
Who showed of old his armour and his gems,
His gold and silver, to the travellers come
From a far country, lead the wanderer on
Through all her treasure-chambers, one by one,
Till nought is left unshown.   Nor shall there fail
Due fruit of knowledge for the use of man ;
The winds shall be his servants, and the fire
Shall do his bidding, and the mighty seas,
Foam-crested, he shall pass : and subtle skill
From out the poor and common elements
Of daily use shall frame a demon-power,
As dread as are the thunderbolts of God ;
And when the nations meet in fierce array,
Armed for the battle, forth from either side,
No more the clouds of arrows and of spears
Shall darken air, and speed on wings of death,
But lightning-flashes, thunder-roars, and smoke
Of myriad forms of horror.
                              Shall it be
That this advance in knowledge will but bring
New strength for evil ?   I have dreamt my dream ;
And still, it seems, there comes, as end of all,
The fiercer discord and the mightier hate.
Shall this be all the progress ?   Shall the world
Mourn over its great failure, as I mourn
The failures of my life ?   I too have grown
In wisdom, yet I droop before my time,

Cut off from all the sweet companionship
Which makes the joy of life ; and evil tongues
Make sport of me, as did the Philistines
Of that strong man in Ashkelon.   To them
I am but as the wizard gaining lore
By spells forbidden, to the demon sold
By solemn compact, mad or mountebank :
And so my mind misgives me it shall be
Throughout the future.   Shall the poison run
Through the long ages of the sons of men,
As now it runs ?   Shall childhood fade away
In foulest shame, the human rosebuds flung
To rot on dunghills, all their fragrance gone,
And all their fair warm hues of Paradise ?
Shall youth still waste its prime of golden hope
In aimless fancies, lowest lusts, that war
Against the soul's perfection ?   Shall the man
Tread backward, downward, from the earlier height
His soaring youth had climbed to, till he stands
On that low level of the stagnant fen,
Where ripening years bring only narrower thoughts,
And clouds and mists shut out Truth's orient light,
And buzzing flies and croaking reptiles drown
The clear calm music of her heavenly voice ?
Shall Love grow colder as the years pass on,
And palsied age creep, muttering, at the grave,
His curses on the future ?   In that time,
Which seemed but now a·golden age renewed,

Shall he who stands above his peers, and sees
More clearly all the order of the world,
Be as I am, the sport of fools, his name
Cast out as evil, hated by the souls
To whom he cleaves in love, with none to share
The secret of his heart?

                  [A voice is heard without chanting a
                        Latin hymn.

                       Ah! there is one
Who sees as yet the tapestry of life,
Its bright side outward, and the notes trill out
Without one touch of any thought but joy.
" *Jam lucis orto sidere*," he sings,
And thinks but of the light that daily brings
Life and its blessings.   I, with wider glance,
See that the star is rising on his soul,
The star of Wisdom, and foretell his life
Shall be but one long pilgrimage, as once
The Magi of the East beheld in heaven
A new and brighter orb, and followed it
They knew not whither.   Shall it lead him on,
Through many wanderings, over moor and rock,
As it led them to where the young Child was?
Yes, I have watched him, as the saint of old
Watched his true son; and since the message came
From him who once had shared my wider thoughts,
And now forgets not, on St Peter's chair,
The poor Franciscan, I have made him mine,

Have taught him, trained him. He, with clearest
    speech,
Can lead the way through all the tangled maze,
Bring out my meaning from behind the veil,
Speak as another self. Fulcodi's soul
Will own him as a brother, look to him,
Young as he is, as one who comes to teach,
The true disciple of the aged seer,
Whose strength is failing. Yet at times my heart
Misgives me. Dare I send him? Shall I thrust
That pure bright life upon the world's rough sea,
And risk its shipwreck?
               [*Voice is heard singing again.*
" *Sint pura cordis intima.*" Ah! boy,
Thou hardly need'st that prayer, so fair and free
That bright young soul ; and yet 'tis well, 'tis well.
Too soon the serpent trails across the blooms,
All virgin in their whiteness, and the taint
Remains, though it be conquered. Yes, pray on,
Sing bravely, and thy work will not descend
To labour for the treasures most men love,
Nor knowledge issue in the fevered thirst,
The wandering doubt, the blank disquietude.

   Enter JOANNES, *a young Franciscan.*
Good-morrow, boy ; thy voice sounds cheerily
Through this cold morning air, as doth the lark's,
When, soaring high in summer's depths of blue,

His carol, though we see him not, still gives
Its witness of his presence.　Thou art glad,
And one whose blood is chilled with age and toil
Welcomes thy gladness.

Joan.　　　　　　　　How should I be sad,
My father, when our God has given me all
The fulness of His favours?　I, who, poor,
Bereaved of father, mother, home, have found
Safe shelter here ; and for the city's crowd,
This saintly calm ; for ignorance untaught,
Uncared for, all the wondrous thoughts that rise
From opening knowledge ; for the ribald scoff
And fierce rough jests, these songs of seraphim,
These prayers by day and night, I must be glad.
But thou, my father, on thy weary brow
Are traced long hours of vigil.　Thou hast watched
The seven-starred Wain move onward till it paled,
And wrapt in thought as in a garment, lost
Thy power to count, or eve, or night, or morn.
Yield now to nature, let me tend on thee,
Prepare thy couch, bring furs to cover thee,
And sing thee to thy slumber.　I must pay
The debt I owe thee.

Bacon.　　　　　　Thanks, thou gentle boy;
Thy kindness saddens, as but now thy song
Gave me a moment's cheer.　What debt is due
For all the little thou hast learnt of me,
The much that thou hast taught me?　Is not life

The brighter for all interchange of thought?
Is it not written, " Freely ye received,
As freely give." 'Twere better rest than sleep,
To talk with thee of Wisdom, and the paths,
Star-paved, that lead to her high firmament,
And give thee counsel how to know the true,
And shun the counterfeit.   Three years have passed
Since first I taught thee.   Does thy purpose cleave
As steadfastly as ever ?   Take account ;
Look back upon the ground that thou hast gained,
The world that lies before thee, and decide
If thou hast courage for thy high emprise.
Should thy heart fail thee, or thy spirit faint,
Turn back to lowlier ways.   Hast thou the sign
God gives His chosen warriors ?   As of old,
Their joys and sorrows are not as the rest :
Their fleece is wet when all around is dry ;
The dew of heaven is theirs, to cheer and bless,
When others sink upon the arid sand ;
Their fleece is dry when all around is wet,
They have their sorrows which the world knows not,
Their conflicts in the midnight loneliness
That others taste not.

    Joan.   Yes, my father, yes.
My heart misgives me not.   Thy hand has helped
My feeble steps through maze and tangled brake,
And I look back on what, when first I came,
Seemed a far country.   All the threefold way

Of Grammar, Logic, Rhetoric, I leave
As childish things behind me, and I press
On to the great Quadrivium, where I know
Thy counsels will not fail me. How I fare
In music thou hast heard. Each day from thee
I learn the mystic powers and subtle laws
Of Numbers; and my hand is skilled to trace
The circles and triangles, whence we learn
To measure earth and heaven. When nightfall comes
I watch the stars, and note where Venus shines,
Companion to the moon, or seen at morn,
The herald of the sun. The Pleiads fair,
Arcturus and Orion, these I know,
And on the silver sphere thy hands have framed
Can trace the line which marks the equal day,
And all the cycles upon cycles turned
That cause the changing seasons; and the eclipse,
That frightens others as the scourge of God,
Disturbs me not, who know that earth and sky
One great Workmaster own; nor when at night
The bearded star o'er half the heaven extends
Its trail of misty light, have I looked on
With more than placid wonder. Yet there lies
One world I have not entered, and all this
Is but the outer court and vestibule
Of God's great temple. I would scan and know
The mysteries of my life—the spirit's life—
Whence come my thoughts, and what the primal
    source

Of all our knowledge, how to judge aright
Amid the strange confusions of our time,
Whence come the truths which subtle skill of art
Builds up into a system. Soon I trust
My progress onward will attain the prize,
And I shall enter on the topmost clime
Of all our knowledge, woo Philosophy,
As bridegroom woos his bride, and passing on
From lower teachers, list to him who speaks
Through all the ages, chief, supreme, the lord
Of many worlds, as he of Macedon,
The pupil of that seer of high renown,
Was lord of many nations. Yes, I crave
To know what he, the Master of the Wise,
Has left as our inheritance ; and then,
When human knowledge rounds itself full orbed,
The outward and the inward universe
Mapped out and planned, to search the things of God,
The treasures of His truth which, hid in Christ,
His Church goes on unfolding, age by age,
The counsels of the past eternities,
The vision of the future, all the power,
The love, the wisdom of the Eternal Three :
This were the crown of all.

  Bacon.   Ah, boy, thou dream'st
As I have dreamt before thee. Now the way
Seems clear and open, and the mountain-height
Far off is radiant with the rosy dawn.

But ere thou reach it, many a weary day
Thou must toil on, and find the pathway rough,
The woods bewildering, seas of ice and snow
Between thee and the summit. And the path
Thou choosest leads astray. It is not thus
That thou can'st climb to wisdom. Not by books,
The dead traditions of a glorious name,
Such as men give thee, can'st thou converse hold
With that Stageirite. I have scanned his words
In his own speech, clear, definite, and bright
As instruments of steel, and I have owned
The might of that far-reaching intellect,
And said within me, "What this man has done,
I too may do, and from his vantage-ground
Go on and conquer." But these friars, who teach,
With vile monks' Latin marring all his thoughts,
Who feed on worthless husks and grainless chaff,
As asses browse on thistles, let them be;
Learn not of them, but go to Nature's self,
And question at her shrine oracular,
And wait her answer. Dogmas of the schools,
Thy master's teaching, yea, thy fondest dreams,
That seem to solve the problems of the world,
Test by her mighty voice, the fact that lives
When man's devices perish. I have toiled
Through painful years, and here alone I find
The way that leads to Truth—and now to-day
I set the seal on this my life's long task:

This volume holds the sum of all I deem
Most worthy of preserving, golden dust
From sands and rock collected.   This shall be
The witness to the future age, of one
Whom few or none acknowledged in his life ;
And one day thou shalt read it, and shalt find
True guidance.   Yet I know not, as I speak,
How I may baffle those that watch and spy,
My brothers, in whose dreams the demon comes
And marks me his.   In very zeal of faith,
Should these poor parchments come into their
        hands,
They will condemn, destroy them, and the fire
Feed on them grimly, while they wish, poor souls,
It had the writer also.   I must take
My measures to defeat them.   One has said,
Christ's Vicar, seated on St Peter's throne,
That he will welcome what I write.   To him
I seek to send it ; but the way is long,
And friends are few. There needs the strength of limb,
The fearless heart, the mind to measure right
The value of the trust, the golden seed
Of a more golden harvest, ere I find
One fitted for a pilgrimage like that.
    Joan. Hast thou not found him, O my father ? Lo,
Though shrinking from mine own infirmity,
Fearless of all besides, myself I give
To do thy bidding.   Did I say but now

I sought to pay my debt, and shall I lose
The occasion that has come, I do not say
To pay it, (that were idle,) but to give
My witness that I owe it?   Suffer me
To bear the priceless casket ; with my life
I answer for its safety.   Next my heart,
As on the heart of Aaron lay of old
Urim and Thummim, it shall lie, the Light
And Truth for future ages.   None shall tear
The treasure from my keeping.   Never child
More safe in mother's arms than that shall be,
Firm in my grasp till death.   I will not trust
Another's hands ; myself will make my way
To where Christ's Vicar, on St Peter's throne,
Sits girt with subject princes.   And my voice
Shall tell him that I bring, not gold or gems,
Rubies or orient emeralds, but one pearl,
Spotless and noble, and that pearl of price,
Thy wisdom, O my father, which thy soul,
Deep diving in the boundless seas of thought,
Hath gained, of many, goodliest.

    Bacon.   Hast thou heard,
Dear dreamer, of the words that bid us heed
How we cast pearls before the beast unclean ?
Those purpled prelates, pampered parasites,
Buffoons, or pedants—thou wilt seem to them
A madman, and thy journey o'er the seas
But a fool's errand.   No.   The way is long,

And thou art young, and I am loth the world
Should deal with thee too roughly, loth to think
The change and chance of travel may wear off
Thy blameless freshness. Wait awhile. 'Tis best
To carry on the purpose of thy life,
And give thy years to wisdom.

    Joan.   Nay, not so ;
God watches o'er the wanderer.   On his head,
Or sleeping on the sultry wastes of sand,
With lions prowling round him, or on height
Of snow-crowned mountains, when the icy wind
Bears the wolf's howling to the frighted sense,
God's angels come and go, and they will keep
My soul from evil.   Trust me, let me go,
For so, my father, (I must tell thee all,)
Thou addest to my debt.   My soul has longed
These many months to see that greater world
That lies beyond the limits of our cells.
Fain would I seek the sepulchres of saints,
And kneel where martyrs conquered, fain would hear
The voices of the wise, and kneeling low
Before the teacher whom the general voice
Has owned Seraphic, (so the love of God
Burns in his soul with clear, enduring flame,)
Learn from him all divinest mysteries.
And Rome itself, the wonder of the world,
The mistress of the Empire and the Church,
City of kings and saints—Rome still has been

My waking dream.   Deny me not, I pray,
Lest I begin to think thou dost not trust
My courage, or my steadfastness of will.
Hast thou not known me?   Have I not obeyed
Thy least command? gone forth at thy behest
At midnight, when the storm was on the hills,
And spectre forms seemed flitting through the air,
To cull thee simples? swum across the flood,
To bear thy letters to thy secret friends,
Thy brothers in the mystery of thine art?
And should I fail thee now?   It must not be.
Thou wilt consent, my father.

  Bacon.   Dare I choose
Between the two resolves?   To say, Go forth,
May risk his life, may mar his innocence ;
And should I hear that evil on the way
Befell him, I shall go down to the grave,
As did the patriarch for his best-loved son,
In dust and ashes ; yet to say, Hold back,
Renounce the bold and perilous emprise,
May quench the fire which God himself has lit,
And crush it into dulness.   And the book,
What then shall come of that ?   It gathers mould
On some high shelf, unread ; or friars, who hate
With all a bigot's hatred, tear its leaves ;
Or ruder hands seize on it, as the work
Of an old wizard, whose accursed spells
Have given their children agues, or have sent

The murrain through their flocks.   No, let me see
In that clear eye God's augury of good,
In that strong voice God's oracle of might ;
And as one said of old, the prophet boy,
To Israel's pontiff, " Here am I, O Lord,
For Thou didst call me," and at last the priest
Knew that it was of God, so I may know
That here is one true servant of the Truth,
Elect before the world to do His will,
And minister to Wisdom.   Were it not
A selfish fear to keep him here with me,
That I may share his gentle ministries,
And find one soul like-minded with mine own ?
I, too, am offering up a sacrifice
On that high altar.   Go, then, boy, go forth ;
God's blessing on thee, and His angels guard
Thy soul from evil.   Once they kept their watch
O'er him who journeyed to Ecbatana,
And that bright vision of the archangel's love
Will not be far from thee.   I will not fail
To watch and pray ; and far as human words
Can help thee on thy way, thou shalt not miss
For highest words of honour.   I will write
To that high Pontiff at whose feet I lay
The long-stored treasures of the mine of thought,
And tell him of thy noble zeal, thy love
For knowledge, worthiest mistress, and for me,
Thy most unworthy master.   Fare thee well ;

If thou must go, 'twere best thou tarry not ;
Our brothers here are lynx-eyed.
    Joan. :   On my knees
I thank thee, father, bless thee ; and I start
This very hour, across the frozen snow,
And track the river's windings.   As I go,
My heart will sing for joy, more blithe and glad
Than when thou heard'st me in the morning's prime.

> [*Exit, and is heard singing :*
>   *Jam lucis orto sidere,*
>   *Deum precemur supplices ;*
> *And again,*
>   *Sint pura cordis intima.*

II.

SCENE—*The same cell in the Franciscan house at Oxford.*
Eve of St Barnabas, A.D. 1294.

ROGER BACON *reclining on a couch.*

ONCE more the same old cell, the gray stone walls,
A little gloomier for the damp of years,
The cobwebs thicker, and the shelves that stood
Above my couch, with books that then I made
The treasure of my life, forbidden lore,
Now stript and bare ; yet still, for all the change,
I breathe more freely here.   These many months

I wearied of the sight that met my eyes,
The moss-grown courtyard and the cloistered walk,
The four high walls that shut the world from view,
While all I did, or waking or asleep,
Was open to espial ; and the friars
Would stand and watch the casement, wondering still
If once again the wizard would return
To his dark arts, with necromantic rod
Call up the dead, or seek the mystic stone,
Transmuting all to gold, or make the stars
Unfold their secrets.   Now at last I rest ;
They know the end is coming, and their hearts
Beat with some touch of pity, conquering fear,
And leave me to myself, to sleep my sleep
Where my sick fancies lead me.   Here, at least,
I look upon the fair green fields, and list
The lowing of the cattle ; and the scent
Of meadow-sweet and cowslips upward floats,
As with a balmy power to soothe and lull
My fevered thoughts ; and lo ! at eve and morn
I see the golden sunlight, and it pours
Some warmth on these old limbs, benumbed and chilled
With long inaction.
                          And the end is near :
I know it by all signs that sages tell,
The dews that gather on the brow, the pulse
Both weak and fitful ; and my wandering thoughts
Go backward o'er the vision of my life,

And the dim past resumes its outlines clear,
Its colours full and strong.   The infant years,
The boy's first striving after name and fame,
The thirst that led me far beyond my peers
To drink deep waters at the wells of Truth ;
The mind that could not rest, by wearing thoughts
Led on and on, to question evermore
All old traditions, living face to face
With Nature and her teaching.   Then a change,
The turning-point of life, when Grosseteste came,
Wise, great, and good, and knowing all my needs,
Bade me renounce the world's bewildering pomps
And join the Brothers, then of world-wide fame,
Bound by the law which he, their Master, gave,
From fair Assisi on the Umbrian hills.
Thou saint of God, whose life to human eyes
Seemed as a madman's folly, and thine end
One without honour, now supremely blest
And numbered with the saints, I may not dare
To sit in judgment on thee.   I have learnt
That lesson now, and wait till that great day,
Revealed by fire, shall try each artist's work,
And manifest its worth.   Enough for me
To know thee true and noble, wide of heart,
And burning with the love that many floods
Of waters quench not.   Others choose their loves
From out the fair and noble, woo and wed
Kings' daughters, or in youth and beauty find

What meets their soul's desire.   Youth's wandering
    dreams
See many forms that beckon it to tread
This path or that.   As once on Ida stood
Three goddess forms in glorious rivalry,
So now they strive for mastery.   Wisdom first,
With clear, calm brow and star-crowned diadem,
And Pleasure with her cup of poisoned wine,
And Power all queenly, with her stately tread
And mighty sceptre ;—thus they came once more
To lead his soul to bondage ; but he made
Far other choice than did the Dardan youth,
And for his bride took one in whom he found
Divine, unearthly beauty, such as wins
The heart to love and worship, but to those
Who look with outward eyes, deformed and grim,
Stript of all form and brightness.   Thee he chose,
Divinest Poverty, and gave to thee
A passionate devotion, such as knight
Gives to the dearest idol of his soul,
A chivalrous allegiance.   As Christ lived,
The Lord and Master in whose path he trod,
So he lived, homeless, wandering, begging bread,
Sharing the peasant's hovel, unabashed
In face of kings and princes, fearing not
To kiss the leprous hand, as one might stoop
In homage to an emperor.   Wondrous heart,
That owned no form of human abjectness

Too low for reverence, and threw down its glove
Before the strong and mighty of the earth,
In stern defiance claiming for the poor
Their portion in the Kingdom.

                          So I judge
At last, but then I measured not thy soul
As now I measure, and with colder heart
I took thy vows.   To me at eve and morn,
In waking dream, or vision of the night,
The face of Knowledge looked from out the clouds
With such a wondrous beauty that I longed
To make her mine for ever.   Nature spread
Her glorious treasures round me, and each path,
Through all her mighty labyrinth, seemed to lead
To that one shrine where Knowledge stood supreme
To crown her worshippers.   What most I loved
Even in our Master was the heart that owned
Its fellowship with Nature.   Mother earth
Was more to him than idle phrase of course ;
The sun was as his brother, going forth
To bless both good and evil ; air and fire
Were near of kin ; and water pure and clear
Was as a sister, stainless as the moon
That walks in brightness.   All the creatures came
Within the compass of his burning love,
His gospel of the Kingdom, and to all
He preached the great glad tidings, would not leave
The birds that sang, the flowers that breathed perfume,

And oped their golden bosoms to the sun,
Till they too joined the wondrous orison,
The mighty JUBILATE.   That to me
Was witness that I might unblamed pursue
My heart's strong master-passion, might embrace,
With all a lover's rapture, the fair form
Of Nature, and behold with wondering eyes
Her full unveilèd beauty.   So I toiled
Through sleepless nights, and days that knew not rest,
Far up the steep ascent, and saw afar
My Queen in all her glory ; so I learnt
The rising and the setting of the stars,
The secret springs of life and its decay,
And moved ahead of all my peers, alone,
Unresting, and unhasting.   This is past ;
My memory fails me, and they slip away,
The dreams and schemes that once were all in all,
As slips a sword from out a sick man's grasp :
Yet still I keep the sense of what has been,
The joy of having known, and own in this
The charm that kept me from the mire and clay
My feet might else have sunk in, yea, a spell
Against the dangers others of my robe
Have found too fatal.   'Twas not wisely done
On all to bind that ecstasy of love
Which revels in privations.   Well for him,
The stainless-hearted knight of poverty,
That wandering through the world as one who lacks

His daily bread, but for the feebler souls
The beggar's life may bring the beggar's thoughts,
The sordid care, the coarse and earthly greed,
The baser that all gloss and finer touch
Are torn away, and nothing left to hide
The swine-like foulness.

                     So my life passed on,
Amid the strife of tongues, and war of sects,
Misjudged, condemned, and the good ground choked
With bitter roots of evil. Some I found
False friends, half-hearted, sharing aims and hopes
Until the winds blew roughly, then afraid
To face the pelting of the storm that beat
All fiercely on me. Some were open foes,
In very zeal for God ; and here and there
Was one whose heart made answer unto mine,
As face meets face from out the crystal stream,
Another, yet the same, whose soul drank in
The wisdom that I gave him, and did grow,
As grow the trees well-watered of the Lord
In Eden's garden. One such faithful soul
I parted from long since, and in the night
Come haunting fears that on my hand there lies
The stain of blood, that I before the Throne
Am guilty of the waste of that fair life.
I sent him forth to brave the evil world,
The dangers of the city and the wild,
And know not of the issue. Did he die

In icy cavern on the Alpine heights ?
Or did the death-sleep fall on weary frame,
The eternal snow his shroud of burial?
Or did the fever smite him in the marsh,
Or robbers strike him down, or lives he still,
Gaining, it may be, wealth and power and fame,
A teacher of the wisdom that I taught,
At Padua or Bologna ? Have the years
Quickened his zeal, till like a two-edged sword
His word goes forth to slay the foes of truth,
Poor wanderers in the darkness ? Darker yet,
Fouler the vision as my thoughts pass on,
Creeps he, as creeps a spaniel, in and out,
Through postern gate, and by-ways of the house ;
A tyrant's minion, whispering at his ear
His scurril jests against the wise and good?
Not that, O God,—send any doom but that !
Yet I have known such downfalls, and the best,
Corrupted, prove the worst ; and I would give
What life still lies before me, rather say,
I would drag on its burden ten years more,
To know him free from evil. Since he went
The days have gone more wearily ; old age
Has chilled the veins, and clouded o'er the skies ;
And, as in penalty for that my sin
Which for my weak pride risked a brother's soul,
Ten dreary years in prison, where the Seine
Flows by the dungeon walls, have tamed my strength.

I am not what I was, and have not found,
All wanderings over, where to plant my feet
Amid these tossings of uncertain seas,
And howlings of the tempest.　Fair outspread
Before the body's eye is that rich sky,
Where clear dark azure slopes to golden blaze,
Through thousand orient, hyacinthine hues,
A very sky of opal ; but within
The heaven is dark, and neither sun nor star
For many days appeareth.　I have lost
My grasp upon the faith my brothers hold :
Their Creeds and Aves cannot stay my soul ;
And the wide thoughts I had of that great Mind,
The life and breathing spirit of the world,
These flit before me cold and colourless,
As spectres of the dead amid the snow,
And have no power to comfort.　Must I pray
His prayer, who, launching out upon the dark
Dim sea of death, thus uttered all his soul :
" My life began in shame, wore on in care ;
Trembling I pass beyond the bourn of earth,
Causa causarum, miserere mei."　·
Oh ! for some voice to bid the spectres flee,
As clear and calm and strong as once I heard
Those parting notes, which come to me at times,
Like music of sweet chimes across a lake,
Or breeze, balm-laden, o'er a dreary sea.
　.　It may not be.　I sigh and moan in vain ;

I die alone ;—through all the vacant air
No speech, no answer.

Enter JOANNES.

              Who is this that comes
So late ?   The dusk of twilight hides from me
Thy face, my brother.   Thou perchance art come,
Anselm, or Francis, at our Prior's behest,
To do the last kind office.   It is well ;
I would not die unhouselled ; ye may claim
That reverence from me.   But as yet no need
For pressing haste ; confession, unction, prayer,
I scorn them not ; but tarry for a while,
Till morning comes again.   For these few hours
Leave me to mine own communings.

  Joan.   For this
I come not, father, am not one of those,
Thy brethren, or thy gaolers, but for love
Of our dear Lord, and memory of past years,
I seek thy cell, have wandered far and wide
To seek it, and at last have found thee here,
Sick, weary, dying, and I fain would pay
A heavy debt of thirty years ago,
And tend thee to the last.

  Bacon.   I thank thee, son,
Whoe'er thou art.   Most debtors are not wont
To have such memories.   Thou, it seems, art one
Who waits not to be asked, but does forthwith

What conscience bids him.   Yet thy task is vain:
What need have I of payment of old debts?
Time was I might have welcomed heaped-up coins,
To help my search for knowledge, wrought at length
The alchemy which, carried to its height,
Had brought me to that quintessence of gold,
Transmuting baser metals, giving life,
With power to heal all sickness.   As I am,
I care not for it, cannot use it.   Keep
Thy money to thyself; or if thou shrink,—
As something noble in thy tone and speech
Warns me thou wilt,—from usufruct of that
Which is not thine, bestow it on the poor;
Search out some scholar, struggling, naked, spent,
And give him food and raiment; clear away
The stones that wound his feet, the briars that tear,
As upward on that steep ascent he climbs,
Where thou hast climbed before him.

    Joan.   Nay, my father,
I speak not of the debt which coin can pay;
I come as one who owes himself to thee,
And must return thine own with usury.
I was that scholar, struggling, naked, spent,
And thou did'st clothe and feed me. Thou did'st snatch
My spirit from the toys of childhood's sense,
My life from off the husks the swine did eat,
And led me on to wider thoughts, a life
Of nobler aims.   Thine ever-watchful eye

Kept my young heart from taint of base desire,
And so I sank not in the graves of lust,
As others sank around me. Can I fail
To own that debt which only God can pay,
And ask thee to take all, my heart, myself?

Bacon. Thy words, my son, wake échoes in the void
Of what was once a heart, with hopes and fears,
The sorrows and the joys which come to all ;
And yet they fail to tell me who thou art.
Through those past years, (thank God, at least, for that !)
I have known many such, have rendered help
To many wanderers—yea, have done my best
To lead them in the bright crystalline path,
In the white robes of God's anointed priests ;
And I have seen on many a lofty brow
The unseen cross that, traced by angel hands,
Marked them as Christ's true soldiers, watched the
    growth
Of knowledge, and the fruit that brings not now
The stern death-sentence, but is fair and sweet,
And pleasant to the eyes, and makes of toil
(For still we eat our bread with sweat of brow)
One life-long Sabbath. Give some token true
By which from out those faces of the past,
All clear and bright, I may discern the one
Which now I know is near, yet cannot see.

Joan. Thou wilt remember, sure, one winter's morn
When one such young disciple went his way

To do thy errand, chanting, as he went,
The hymn that thou had'st taught him.   So he sang,
Thy words of blessing ringing in his ears,
>   " *Sint pura cordis intima,*
>   *Absistat et vecordia."*

And thus he poured his matin orison—
>   " *Jam lucis orto sidere,*
>   *Deum precemur supplices."*

Bacon.   God gives
His answer to my passionate complaint ;
I see thee then at last.   Thou hast not failed
To bring the golden promise of thy youth
Up to its full perfection.   Still thy voice
Speaks of thine inner life ; thy music comes
Clear, strong, and manly, as of old it came,
And wakes, as then, an echo in my heart,
Till now too long in silence.   Wondrous power
Of that high strain of noble minstrelsy
Our fathers left us, holiest thoughts to stir,
Joy's rapture, and the hush of solemn fears !
We lose the power by all our petty aims,
Our boyish tricks of art.   We hear not now
That grand old music, but the voice untrue,
The mock falsetto, thrills through ear and brain,
Melting, not strengthening.   Thou, I see, art still
True to thy master ; still thou pressest on
Through worthiest paths to highest excellence.
Ah ! could we gain the height, and search the depth

Of that dread secret of the might of sound,
Who knows but man, in harmony with God,
Might learn the music which the angels love,
The concord of the starry heavens that move
Melodious in their courses, join with them
In that great hymn which rises evermore
From all creation, use God's gift of song,
With Orphic power to tame the stubborn beast,
To stop the wild bird in its swift-winged flight,
To charm the venomed serpent, and stand up,
With all things in subjection at his feet,
Lord of a world in order.   So should man
Come to his brother man with power to soothe
All sorrow, purify each low desire,
Illumine clouded vision.   Here would be
The true elixir ; Age itself would lose
Its·pain, its weakness, soothed and lulled to rest
By that divinest music, and would find
The discord of its life attuned and hushed
In that its Euthanasia.   So, of old,
The minstrel-boy who stood before the king,
Through all the madness found the human soul,
Sang to it of the deeds of heroes old,
The wonders of the outstretched arm of God,
The marvel and the mystery of His love,
And brought it back to life ; so, nearer still
To what has passed but now, the gray-haired seer,
His vision failing, and prophetic pulse

C

No longer beating quickly, bade one fetch
A minstrel youth to stir the ebbing life,
And then gave forth his counsel. So, my son,
I list to thee with thrillings of the heart,
Each nerve in tension. Ere the hour be past,
Ere age resumes its weakness, and cold mists
Of dim oblivion shroud me, tell thy tale,
The story of thy life. Through these long years
My heart has been with thine, and I have wrought
(Fancy still working in my waking dreams)
Whole epics for thee, full of noblest deeds,
Thyself the hero—sometimes, unawares,
Have glided into thoughts of darkest doom,
And seen thy life a tragedy to chill
The very blood with horror. Now, at last,
The poet's work is done, and thou wilt tell
What goes beyond it all. I long to hear
How fared it with thee, how with that thy trust
I thought so much of then, but now have learnt
To leave in other hands.

 Joan.   I will not tell—
Thou wouldst not wish it—all the varied scenes
Through which my life has led me : cities old,
Dark forest glooms, or mountain heights of snow,
Wide plains, all golden with the waving corn,
Or fair hill-sides, where climbs the purpling vine.
Enough, I reached my goal. At Rome's great gate
I stood, and there, in presence of her lord,

Vicar of Christ, stood trembling.   In his hands
I placed the treasure I received from thee,
And did mine office truly.
   Bacon.   Ah! and then . . .
What said he?   Did he commune much with thee?
Learn of thee what the parchments could not tell?
Take counsel how to work the mighty change
I set before him?   Which of all the three
Seemed most to stir him?   Death, I know, cut off
Completion of my hopes; but I were glad
To know he shared them.
   Joan.   'Tis not mine to tell
The secrets of his purpose.   All I heard
Were some few words of kindness.   He rejoiced
To hear that thou wert free.   It grieved him sore
When knowledge brought but sorrow.   If I stayed
In Rome, he hoped to see me.   Then he took
Thy crystal sphere, and poised it in his hand,
And smiled to see the bending of the rays,
The point that kindled fire—"These things were
    strange,
And it was well some men should care for them,
And give the world amusement.   For thy books,
He would ere long, when pressing cares of state,
And holier duties left him time enough,
Give them some hours of leisure."   That was all.
Nay, nay, my father, grieve not.   So the world
Runs on : its fame, its favours, will not stay

The spirit in the Judgment.   Well for thee
The reed broke down and pierced thee.
   Bacon.   Was that all ?
No care for thee, no honour, no support,
High office, state of teacher, as I asked?
   Joan. Some few months passed, and now and then
     there came
A kindly smile, and then I saw no more.
He died, and I was left in Rome alone,
A stranger, friendless.   And my soul was sick
To see and hear the words and deeds of men
In that great city.   Where the church should be
At oneness with itself, were strife and hate ;
Where I had hoped to find Jerusalem,
City of peace, and peopled with the good,
The pure, the pitiful, the meek, I found
But Sodoma and Babel.   Lust and hate,
Time-serving greed, and wisdom of the schools
Well-tuned for princes' favour ; what was this
To one whom thou had'st trained to nobler thoughts ?
Weary of life, I turned away, and wiped
The very dust of that accursed place
From off my feet, and in my sorrow sought
A refuge elsewhere.   So, for seven long years
I journeyed through those old Italian towns,
And sat and listened as the teachers gave
Their stores of knowledge to the wondering crowd.
And here again, my father, thou had'st spoiled

Thy pupil for the common grooves of life.
I learnt from thee to face the living fact,
To question Nature, bow before her throne,
And do her heartiest homage.   There I found
One name in Nature's place, enthroned supreme,
Words changing place with things, and all engrossed
With subtle weaving of their cobweb thoughts,
As if their barren logic would unlock
The store of Nature's wonders.   Most of all,
My heart was faint and weary when I heard
The words they spake of God.   Thy loving care
Had led me to the fount of heavenly truth,
The very words of prophet, psalmist, saint,
Of One above them all ; and I had owned
Their power to quicken.   Now I found those words
Forgotten, lost, misrendered; jangling talk,
Words without knowledge, darkening counsel, husks
Not even swine could feed on.   Darker yet,
Where'er I went I heard thy name reviled :
The man whom I had known as father, friend,
Whose sheltering hand had guarded me from taint,
And taught me truth in all things ; he it was
Whom every teacher warned his flock against
As heretic, magician, infidel ;
And when I spake thy name men frowned on me,
Shrank from my contact, counselled me to go
Lest evil should befall me.   Most of all,
The brothers of our Order vexed my soul,

Condemning thee unheard.   The man whose words
I fondly deemed seraphic, from whose lips
I hoped to drink the untainted stream of life,
Stood forth as thy accuser.   Soon I heard
Of thy long, hopeless exile, sought in vain
Admission to thee, where by Notre-Dame
The Seine flows swiftly ; then, perplexed and sad,
Went forth once more a wanderer through the world.
   Bacon. Was it then so ?   I deemed myself bereaved
Of help and pity ; and thy hand was near
That might have soothed my anguish, and thy voice
Ev'n within ear-shot.   Once indeed I thought
Through the cold stillness of a midnight air
Came floating sounds of sweetest minstrelsy,
The sounds of that old chant of Merton's choir
I taught thee long ago, and then it passed,
And I awoke and found it but a dream.
Wert thou then near, and did thy prayers go up
For him who pined in loneliness ?   At least
Thou hast found comfort.   Voice and words declare
Thou art not now perplexed, but speak'st as one
Who sees his way distinctly, knows the law
That governs all his life, and needs not now
The help of human friend.   How came it so ?
What teaching led thee from thy dull despair,
And gave thee comfort ?
   Joan.   Wandering, as I said,
I came to where the broad and stately Rhine

Flows by Colonia.   There it chanced I met
A brother of our Order, one who said
He knew thee, loved thee.   Not from him I heard
The trite reproach, the worn-out calumny :
He spake as one whose eyes had looked thee through,
And seen thy strength and weakness.   To that man
(Bertholdt his name, he came from Regensburg)
I owe my second self.   Like him who found
The traveller robbed and naked on the way,
Bound up his wounds, and poured in oil and wine,
So he stretched forth the hand of brotherhood,
And led me, poor and weary as I was,
Foot-sore, and spent with travelling through the waste,
Beneath the shadow of the Eternal Rock.

   Bacon. Bertholdt !   I knew him well long years ago.
He preached at Paris, and his words came straight
As arrows to their mark.   Whilst others prosed,
Begging or borrowing, when they dared not steal ;
While bishops droned o'er postills trite and poor,
And chaplains drowsed o'er thread-bare homilies,
His work was true and living.   As of old
The prophets spake and read the thoughts of men,
Revealing all their secrets, so he spake,
And all my soul was kindled for a while,
And my heart flowed in love.   But other things
Came in to mar the friendship thus begun :
That higher wisdom which I then pursued,
The working out that scheme of perspective,

The digging up those roots of Hebrew speech—
This hindered our communion.

 Joan.   Ah! he told
With tears that story. Bear with me, I pray,
If I speak somewhat boldly, telling thee
What words he uttered. "One there was," he said,
"Whom God chose out, elect above the rest,
A vessel of His truth,—the spirit clear,
The heart untainted, patience to endure,
And faith to move the mountain, courage true,
With no respect of persons,—all are his,
Each gift of high, commanding intellect :
Yet lacks he one thing." And when I, amazed,
Looked wondering what defect or secret sin
His vision had detected, so he spake—
" Lacks one thing only, but that one is all :
God's kingdom and the righteousness thereof.
To live in Love ; to see the Father's will,
That forms and rules the secrets of our life ;
To count all knowledge, wisdom, mysteries,
As poor and trifling, Love alone supreme ;
To see that Love throughout the world, and find
A central oneness in the heart of life,
Using each moment for the praise of God,
The good of men, our brothers :—this he needs
Before he finds completeness. Such a soul
God will not leave to sink in slothful ease,
But goad it on, nor leave it peace or rest,

Till it too learns at last how hard it is
To kick against the pricks."

   Bacon.   Thy voice is changed,
My son, since last we met.   Time was when thou
With wondering eyes would'st look upon my face
With faith approaching worship.   Then I seemed
Thy one true teacher.   Now it seems thou own'st
Another as thy master.   Be it so.
So runs the world, as thou did'st say but now.
The old withdraw ; thou lookest for their place,
And find'st them nowhere.   This, at least, I boast :
I sowed the seed, though others reap the fruits ;
I laboured ; they have entered on my toil.

   Joan. Nay, father, 'tis not that I love thee less,
But, as thou taughtest, love the truth yet more,
 That thus I speak.   I come to pay my debt :
Thou gav'st me knowledge of the things of earth,
The wonders of this mighty universe ;
I bring thee knowledge of the things of God,
The peace that passeth knowledge.   Hear my tale,
The witness as of one who once was blind
And now sees clearly.   Bertholdt's words of love
First drew me to him, yes, his love for thee ;
And so I stayed and listened.   Soon I found,
Strange contrast to the evils of the world,
Till then unknown, a life of grace and truth,
Labour, and love, and peace, and purity,
As from a clear bright mirror, giving back

The image of the glory of the Lord ;
A life like Christ's, although no prints of nails
Marked hands or feet.   There all the juggling tricks,
The schools' dead logic, tangled subtleties,
Were heard no longer.   O'er the living Word,
Needing no senses mystic, secret, dark,
They prayed and pondered.   One I heard had spent
Full forty years upon it, and declared
He stood but as a child upon the shore
Of Truth's eternal ocean.   So their life
Steered clear, amid the tempests of our time,
Of shoal and whirlpool.   Poor they were indeed,
But did not make their poverty their boast,
Nor serve it as an idol.   Daily bread
They gained by daily work, and of their own
Gave to the poor around them.   Books they had,
Not scorning, nor o'erprizing, and they taught
The young, as thou did'st teach.   And when the plague
Swept sore among the nations, they were seen
Fearless, unshrinking, healing, if God willed,
Or else consoling.   By the sick man's bed
They knelt and prayed in living words of power,
The Eternal Spirit's utterance.   Music there
Was no poor art to kindle vague desire,
Nor pride and glory of a minstrel's skill,
In hall or bower, or high cathedral choir,
But God's great gift for building up His Church.
There found I all thy words had made me dream :

They went, those brothers, and with holiest hymns,
Not Latin only, such as clerks admire,
But in that native speech of Almaine towns,
The sick and dying roused to thoughts of hope ;
And so they too made answer to the song ;
Their own best thoughts were echoed to their ears,
And e'en the poorest heard the glad good news
Of God's great Kingdom.

    Bacon.   It is well, my son,
As night's dark shadows fall upon my life,
That I should see the brightness of a dawn
Upon the night of nations.   All my life
Such dreams have come before me, but they seemed
Like palaces of Gods, that men have seen
Far off upon the mountains ; pleasant climes,
Isles of the blessed, on a purple sea,
Where sinks the sun in ocean.   Now, behold,
They come in living forms, mine eyes have seen,
Ear heard, hands felt them.   Did I say but now
Thy voice had kindled old prophetic fires ?
Lo ! the fire burns, and will not be restrained.
I see in this thou tell'st me what will grow
Through all the ages.   There the word of life
Falls on the good ground, and it will not fail
Of plenteous harvest, though another reap
What ye are sowing.   O'er this land of ours,
This England, torn by fiercest strife of blood,
This city of fair waters, where, as yet,

Men wage in darkness ceaseless strife of tongues,
The truth shall travel freely.   Yes, from thee,
From those thy helpmates in the life of God,—
Your names forgotten ; by-words of reproach
Heaped on you by your tyrants,—there shall spring
Wide blessings for the world.   The age to come,
Of which I see the promise clear and bright,
Like yon fair streaks which in the distant East
Tell of the day-star's dawn, shall do the work
To which your hands were set, and men shall own
In you the first to light the lamp of truth,
To give the promise of a Church renewed,
A life at one with God.   In that blest hope
I die at peace.   I shall not see those days ;
But as the seer stood once on Pisgah's height,
Looking on plains and rivers, woods and hills,
All Jordan's windings, Shechem's pleasant vale,
Fair Carmel in the west, so stand I now
Upon my watch-tower, and behold in faith
The King in all His beauty, with His Bride,
Bright as the eternal morning.   So I find
My own poor life transfigured.   If I look
Back on the past, I see but wasted years,
The vexing wanderings of a vain research
For things that did not profit.   All my cry
In hour of death, and at the judgment seat,
Were I to gaze upon that past alone,
Would be but one long wailing of despair :

"O Lord our God! we sin exceedingly;"
But He, the King, forgives me all that debt,
And in the ocean of His tideless love
I plunge, and rise, new-born, to higher life,
And the low moan gives way to songs of praise,
As when the elders round the golden throne
Cast their bright crowns upon the crystal sea.
So peace has come at last.

        [Falls back in a trance.

 Joan.   God's love be praised,
I have not come in vain. The prayers are heard
That rose at morn and eve, on stormy seas,
Or where red watch-fires light the tented field.
I thought to lull his weary frame to sleep
With soft low murmurs of an anthem sweet,
That I have known bring brightness to the eyes
Of wounded soldiers in their fevered pain,
And lepers in their lazar-house. My voice
He needs no more. Our God upon his soul
Hath poured the floods of music mightier far
Than our poor skill can dream of. Let Him end
What thus He has begun. ·

 Bacon.   Draw near, my son;
The hour is past, and that unwonted strength—
The flashing of the beacon ere it die—
Has left me faint and feeble. Eyes are dim,
Voice fails me, and the dews of death are chill.
Yet lift me; draw my couch from out the shade

Close to yon casement.   I would fain behold
In the far East, once more, that orient blaze,
That vision of the glory of the Lord,
The token of the Love that streams alike
On evil and on good.   Yes, fair and bright,
This crowning glory of the circling year,
This bright midsummer morn of Barnabas !
Well hast thou timed thy journey, faithful friend,
True son of comfort !
                    [*Joannes moves him to the window.*
                    Lo ! the shadows flee ;
The glory of the Presence comes apace
With healing on its wings ! the golden light
Floods all the azure of that sapphire sea !
Jam lucis orto sidere !   At last
The day-star has arisen !
                                        [*Dies.*

    Joan.   So I close
The eyes that now have seen the Light of Life,
And make once more my lonely pilgimage,
And track once more the windings of the stream ;
The same old burden still upon my lips—
Sint pura cordis intima.
                                        [*Exit.*

AUGUSTINE.

In Memoriam Adeodati.[1]

———◆———

I.

I BOW before the stroke : 'tis right.
   God gave the joy ; He takes away ;
   I hailed the dawn of that clear day ;
I own the Love that brings the night.

That voice so clear in grief or joy,
   That eye that shone like morning's dew,
   That cloudless glance serene and true,
The mother smiling through the boy,—

All these are gone, the nameless grace,
   Quick questions on a thousand things,
   The thoughts that rose on eagles' wings,
To meet the Father face to face.

That voice I ne'er shall hear again,
   Nor feel soft grasp of youthful hand;
   I wander on the lonely strand,
And dreary is the aching pain.

Heir of my sin, conceived in shame,
   Thou gav'st him, Lord, a little while;
   I joyed to watch his infant smile;
Thine all the love, mine all the blame.

"God-given;" so I named him then,
   The child that taught me how to love,
   And spoke of Him who reigns above,
Great Father of the sons of men.

Then first from out the mire and clay
   Of sensuous will, defiling all,
   I rose, and from the abysmal fall
Took one step on to perfect day.

And she, poor lost one, whom my heart
   Loved madly in its strong desire,
   Through travail-pangs, through cleansing fire,
Passed to a mother's holier part.

She left me, and I know not now
   Where roam her feet on Afric's shore;
   But this I know, that evermore
Through life's long years she keeps her vow.

None other wins her love ; but still
   She breathes my name in every prayer,
   And through the calm of midnight air
Strange, wandering thoughts her memory fill ;

Thoughts of the days, long years ago,
   With love's first dawning bright and fair;
   Thoughts of the parting, hard to bear,
Which bowed her to the dust in woe.

Sees she, perchance, when purple eve
   Glows on yon green Atlantic slopes,
   Dim visions wrought of shadowy hopes,
Where joys with terrors interweave ?

Dreams she of him, her darling boy,
   In dawn of manhood's golden prime,
   Still measuring out the lingering time,
With all a mother's pride and joy?

Or floats there now, with whispering breath,
   The word that chills her blood with fear,
   " Weep, mother, weep ; he is not here ;
The boy thou lovest sleeps in death ?"

Or comes his form in radiant sheen,
   As are the angels round the throne,
   To bid her cease her wailing moan,
And join him in the life unseen ?

D

So play I with my sorrow; so
    I paint life's canvas o'er and o'er,
    Like one who, on a lonely shore,
Sees cloudland pictures come and go.

It may be she her course hath run,
    And found her rest, her refuge there,
    Transfigured, purified, and fair,
The mother waiting for her son.

It may be now, in Eden's bowers,
    Her hand in his is fondly prest,
    And she, in blessing doubly blest,
Rejoices through the eternal hours.

II.

Oh, wondrous day of joy and fear!
    Strange sight! the father and the son
    Prepare the self-same race to run,
In snow-white garments drawing near

To where the clear baptismal stream
    Shall wash the scars and stains of earth,
    True token of a holier birth,
True answer to each yearning dream.

We knelt, one foul with years of sin,
    A heart with guilt's dread burden faint,
    And one as free from fleshly taint
As are the souls that Eden win.

They plunged him in the cleansing wave ;
    I watched the angel-face with fear :
    " Ah ! could the world that young heart sear,
Would God that stream could prove thy grave !

" Ah, what, if lusts of ripening youth,
    Sin's poison running through the blood,
    Should whelm thee in the foul, dark flood,
And part thee from the eternal Truth ?

" What, if thy father's guilt in thee
    Should mar the life which thus begins ;
    If bruised and crushed by countless sins,
In vain thou strugglest to be free ?

" Not that, O Lord ! My guilt I own,
    Yet hear a father's eager prayer ;
    That woe were more than I could bear ;
Oh, hear me from Thy mercy's throne !

" I fear lest thoughts that wander wide
    Should mar the simple child-like trust ;
    Lest he, the sin-born heir of dust,
Should speak high words of soaring pride.

" The times are dark, and o'er us sweep
    All forms of evil, dread and dim;
    What if their false dreams over him
With cold, benumbing spell should creep ?"

" What if the cross on stainless brow
    That binds him still to warrior's zeal,
    Faith's token true, life's solemn seal,
Should witness of a broken vow ?"

So prayed I then, and dare I mourn
    The prayer was offered not in vain;
    Or thankless of the love complain,
Which meets my life at every turn.

Though dark are all the future years,
    Though child and mother both are gone,
    Through cloud and mist Thou leadest on;
Thy bow through all the storm appears.

No stain is on the blameless soul;
    No discord mars the angel-voice;
    Thou bidd'st him evermore rejoice;
Thy waves of rapture o'er him roll.

" God-given !"   Yes, Thou tak'st Thine own,
    The angel presence might not stay;
    Through shadows of life's little day
It passes onward to the Throne.

III.

And thou, my mother, thou did'st claim
   My child as thine ; thy constant prayer,
   That saved me from my blank despair,
Rose up for him on wings of flame.

Thou saint, whose vision upward soared
   Through clouds, and skies, and æther far,
   And still beyond or sun or star
Went on and on to seek thy Lord ;

Thou did'st not scorn his prattling ways,
   The lispings of his baby-speech,
   " From such lips often," thou would'st teach,
" Our God has perfected His praise."

When we, with searchings vain perplext,
   No pathway through the clouds could see,
   One word from him, one smile from thee,
Could draw us from our wanderings vext.

So went his whole heart out to thee,
   Thou mother of his new-born life ;
   Through childish moods, through youthful strife,
The skies of home were clear and free.

He loved to hear thy gentle voice
　　Tell tales of saints and martyrs old,
　　Christ's heroes, noble, pure, and bold,
The servants whom He bids rejoice.

He loved to swell the anthem clear,
　　At dawn of day or setting sun,
　　And when his childhood's task was done,
Lie down in slumber, free from fear.

Thy last hour came ; thy glazèd eye
　　Through gathering mists saw Eden's bowers ;
　　We counted all the lingering hours ;
We felt the pulse ; we watched the sigh.

Then came the end.　Thy rest was calm ;
　　The peace of God spread o'er thy brow ;
　　The lips, pressed tight in pain but now,
Smiled sweetly, as though dews of balm

From Eden dropped on fevered frame,
　　And soothed the pang of struggling breath,
　　And through the brooding gloom of death
Clear gleams of Heaven's own brightness came.

But he, poor boy, to whom the sight
　　Of death was full of terrors strange,
　　Who dimly felt the awful change,
Nor rose above the child's affright,—

He cried a loud and bitter cry,
   He wept above the lifeless form,
   He sobbed, till sorrow's rushing storm
Had melted into calmer sigh.

And now they meet: the months have flown,
   And o'er him spread the wings of God.
   I bow before the chastening rod ;
They kneel, adoring at the Throne.

They kneel and pray for me who live,
   That I through all the strife with sin,
   Though flesh and heart should fail, may win
And wear the crown Thy hands shall give.

I kneel and pray for those who rest,
   The mother-saint, the angel-boy,
   That they may pass through circling joy
To yon clear Vision of the Blest,

February 1865.

EVIL-MERÔDACH.

———◆———

THEY led him forth, pale, weak, and bent with age ;
  And though 'twas but the twilight of the dawn,
His eyes, long wont to scan the dungeon's gloom,
From that first glow of orient rose shrank back,
And quivered into darkness.   Little heed
To that loud murmur of the whispering crowd,
To pointed finger, telling or of scorn,
Or kindlier wonder, gave he as he went ;
And ever, when they called him by his name,
"Coniah, King of Judah," still he walked
As though he heard not, passed by loftiest towers,
Where Bel's proud temple rears its winding height ;
Where wide Euphrates sweeps its lordly flood
By quay and terrace ; and the sculptured forms,
Man's face of majesty, and eagle's wings,
And lion's strength, in one strange vision blent,
Guard the great gates, where, hung on terraced slopes,
The rose and myrtle bring to Babel's walls

The brightness and the bloom of Median hills;
And still no look of wonder lit his eye,
No burst of gladness issued from his lips.
Through palace-gates they led him, up the steps
Where porphyry columns prop the marble roofs,
And then to that fair chamber which the king
In pity had assigned him; and they spake,
"Rest here, O prince! The land is glad to-day,
The days of mourning ended! He is gone
Who smote the nations with the scourge of God,
The builder of our city. Many a year
We watched the brooding darkness of his soul,
The madness as of one from whom is gone
His human heart, and all the bestial sense
Usurps dominion; and on every face
There gathered clouds of blackness. Now his reign
Is over. Low in dust that mighty form
Is laid, and on his wondrous throne of gold
Merôdach sits, and nearest at his side
Stands Belteshazzar; and his reign begins
With princely mercy. Lo! from prison dark
He lifts thee up, and bids thee dwell with him,
His guest and friend."
                    And so they took their leave.
Long time he sat, and watched the roseate morn
Glow into gold; looked out upon the ships
Weighed low with precious freightage; heard the clang
Of cymbals and of tabrets, as they marched,

The king's Immortals, through the open plain,
Their golden helmets glittering in the sun.
Beneath him lay the queen's fair paradise,
Where Lebanonian cedars flung their shade,
And bright-eyed stags on fresh, green meadows roamed,
And breath of roses scented all the air ;
Yet still he sat, as though the prison's chill
Clung round him like a mantle ; not the notes
Of martial music, nor the balmy breeze,
Roused him from silence.   Then at last there came
Across the river, from the further shore,
Borne by the wind, sweet sound of broken song,
Sad tones of wailing and of low lament
From captive minstrels.   Where the willows hang
Their weeping branches o'er the lordly stream,
They mourned o'er Judah, waste and desolate,
The vine uprooted, and the vineyard spoiled,
The Temple plundered, desecrate, destroyed,
The golden pride of fair Jerusalem.
And then the king was moved, and falling tears
Told of re-opened fountains ; and there came
The rushing flood of earlier memories,
When from the House, all holy, beautiful,
Such songs rose sweetly, and the hills around
Gave echoes to the winds.   One only sound
He heard not now.   On Babel's homeless shore
They might not lift their Hallelujah chant,
Nor in that strange land breathe Jehovah's songs.

So passed the hours.   That weeping broke the spell
That long had frozen all the springs of life,
And the thick cloud that hung o'er brain and soul
Was touched with gleams of brightness.   Still he sat
Through morn and noon, and spake not.   Then at eve
They came once more, those eunuchs of the court,
With purple robe and kingly chain of gold,
And bade him rise and follow to the hall
Where great Merôdach sat in revelry,
And blazing cressets, with their golden light,
Mocked the still crimson sunset.   Captive kings,
All clad in scarlet, each with chain of gold,
Stood round him, but above them all he placed
The gray-haired exile.   And the two who sat
In highest honour at the king's right hand,
(The one great chief of all the seers except,)
Themselves of David's lineage, Meshach wise,
And Abed-nego, gave him welcome there,
And bade him thank the king, to whom he owed
His new-born freedom.
                            And the king himself,
With priceless goblet from the Temple's stores,
Filled with rare wine from Syria's purpling hills,
Gave him to drink.   And then, the spicèd draught
Quickening the pulse, and pouring warmer life
Through vein and nerve, he opened lips long sealed,
And the slow words came trembling :
                            " Wonder not,

O king, at this my silence.   Many a year
Has passed since human voice, in greeting kind,
Has fallen on mine ear.   And lo ! the song,
The speech, the laugh, bewilder.   Send me back
To that dark silence of the lonely cell,
And let me pass away when God shall call,
And lay my bones in peace.   If I might ask
One favour, I would pray that thou would'st send,
All swathed in spice, with skill of Egypt's sons,
This poor worn frame, that I at last may sleep
Where sleep my fathers, upon Kidron's slope."
   And then the king made answer, " Nay, not so ;
Our reign begins with freedom, mirth, and joy ;
Our glory is to open prison doors,
· And set the prisoners free.   We love to hear
The mourner's thanks, the captive exile's joy.
Therefore make merry.   Here thy life is set
In regal chamber, and among the kings
That eat at this my table, none shall be
In higher place than thou.   Great David's heir
Deserves this honour."
                            "Ah ! that name recalls,"
Then spake Coniah, "years of long ago,
When I too reigned, in name at least, a king,
And dwelt in ceilèd houses where the walls
Were bright with scarlet, and the cedarn roof
Glowed in the sunset, and the voice of mirth
Re-echoed loud, and princes bade me trust

In Egypt's power, and prophets chanted still
Their burdens of the fall of Babylon
In two short years, and priests in stately robes
Bade me be sure the Temple of the Lord
Should stand for ever, and great David's throne
Endure through all the ages. And I stand
Unthroned before thee, and the Temple lies
Low in the dust, deserted ; and where once
The Lord sat throned between the Cherubim,
Prowl fox and boar, and on the altar-stones
The swallow builds her nest. Ah ! one there was,
Whom then we scorned, the seer of Anathoth,
Whose words we little heeded. Now they ring,
Yea, they have rung through all these weary years,
Their knell of doom. And lo ! in childless age,
The idol fallen from its lofty shrine,
Despised and broken, all my glory gone,
A man that has not prospered in his days,
I stand before thee. From His own right hand
God plucked the signet where His name was stamped,
And hurled it into darkness. I have learnt
The lesson of the sorrow and the shame,
And through the dimness of the dungeon's gloom
A light has shone around me, and I see
God's way more plainly. Lo ! He bringeth down
The souls uplifted in their pride of strength :
My father sinned ; the poor and needy came,
The widow and the orphan at his gate

Sat suppliant, all in vain : his years were spent
In one wild revel.   And there came on him
Hard doom of exile, over frozen heights
Of Hermon's passes, over scorching sands ;
Naked the form once clad in purple robes,
And bare the feet once sandalled daintily,
He, buried with the burial of an ass,
Was cast, I know not whither.   Then I came,
Rash, heedless, blind, and dreamt my fevered dreams,
Until the rude awakening.   And for thee,
O king, and for thy city, there awaits
Like desolation.   Now thy mirth is free,
And all the stir and state that meet the eye
In this rejoicing city glad thine heart ;•
And thou, the heir of all thy father's fame,
Forgettest all the lesson of his life.
He too looked out upon the golden towers,
The palaces and gardens, and his soul
Was lifted up, and in his mood of pride
Spake madly, " Is not this great Babylon
Which I have builded ?"   And for that his sin
For five long years he lost his light of life,
The soul that scans the present and the past,
That looks before and after ; and he roamed
All haggard, wild and fierce, in open field,
As on him fell the sunshine and the rain,
Or lurked in den or cavern.   And I see,
O king ! e'en now, as in the northern sky,

The cloud that, rising, spreading, darkening all,
Shall shroud the heaven in blackness, and bring on
The fierce wild whirling of the angry winds,
The floods of many waters ! Woe for thee,
If then thy house is built upon the sands !
For lo ! there comes—(ask thou the seer who sits
At thy right hand ; who, when thy father reigned,
Interpreted his visions ;)—lo ! there comes
A righteous King, anointed of the Lord,
The Shepherd who shall guide the wandering flock,
And ope the gate, and set the captives free.
From Elam comes he, and in purer faith
Than Nineveh and Babel own as theirs,
Shall bow before the God of earth and heaven,
And be His willing servant. Not for him
Thy sculptured idols and thy marble shrines,
But on the holy heights of mountain-top
He greets the one bright witness of his God,
The sun that walks in glory. Few the years
That yet remain, and then thy kingdom falls,
And, courier meeting courier, one shall tell
His tale of woe, ' Great Babylon is lost ! '
And Judah's sons shall own the heathen king,
And he shall bid them seek their father's home,
And rear again on Zion's holy hill
The temple of their God. I shall not see
That day of gladness ; but a little space
Is left me of the weary years of life,

. And little reck I whether, turning back
To yonder prison dark and foul, I die,
Unknown, unwept, with none to wail for me:
' Ah Lord!' and ' Ah, his glory!' or abide
As now, among thy captive princes chief, ·
In mockery of grandeur.   Come what may,
The years have taught their lesson, and mine age
Is wiser than mine youth.   I wait the end:
The fear of God rests ever on my soul;
And so my soul is patient.   Thou, O king,
Be warned in time!"

       He spake; nor did our king,
Merôdach, as we looked for, flash in wrath,
Or kindle into burst of tempest rage,
But first a cloud passed over eye and brow,
And then the wine that sparkled in the gold
He quaffed in haste; and once again his eyes
Were bright and clear, and, reckless in his mirth,
He made his answer—

       " Well then, be it so!
While yet we live we make the most of life,
And crown our brows with rosebuds, ere the rose
Be withered by the sunshine or the frost.
We eat and drink, and if to-morrow's dawn
Bring death, we meet it as a king should meet.
Go thou, old man, who bring'st that spectral form
To scare us at our banquets.   Go thy way;
We will not harm thee, are not wroth with thee,

Thy prison-life has left on thee its gloom,
And bitter woes have vexed thee.   Sleep thy sleep,
Live out thy years.   While mighty Babel stands,
Our feasting shall not fail us."
                              Then his guaids
Once more led out the heir of David's throne.
Slowly and sad he went, nor turned he back,
Nor answer made : but still his long white hair
Flowed round him like a mantle, and he passed
The line of princes to the brazen gates,
His eye lit up with something of the fire
Which speaks of prophet's visions, and his steps
Went onward to the darkness.

March 1865.

THE QUEEN OF THE SOUTH.

I.

THE DEPARTURE.

COME, gather robes of every hue,
 The spikenard and the spice,
The orient sapphire's kingly ray,
 The pearl of costliest price ;
Rich armlets wrought with rarest skill,
 With gems encrusted o'er,
And golden cups, thrice tried in fire,
 From Ophir's palm-girt shore.

Lead forth the camel, let him sail,
 Fit ship for sea of sand ;
The war-horse, let his prancing hoof
 Re-echo through the land ;
Let Sheba's sons around their Queen
 Shout songs of noblest praise,
And bear to distant shores our fame,
 The pride of ancient days.

My princes ! . . . lo, they come ! each one
   In form and state a king,
From Dedan's valleys, myrrh and gold
   And frankincense they bring ;
Their swarth brows wear the diadem,
   Their mantles sweep the ground,
The girdle, wrought with goodliest work,
   In broidered folds goes round.

My seers, the masters of the wise,
   They follow in my train ;
They walk in Wisdom's star-paved way,
   A starry crown to gain ;
Their white hair falls o'er lofty brow,
   They speak with words of power,
And o'er them sweeps, in vigil late,
   The wild, prophetic hour.

Come all, we journey through the world,
   We leave our state and throne,
We cross rough seas and mountains hoar,
   And seek a land unknown ;
We go, the heirs of heroes old,
   To guard their glorious name,
To prove, in sight of man and God,
   Their yet unequalled fame.

For lo! these strangers vex our souls,
  The men of Hiram's ships;
But we will show their vauntings vain,
  False words from lying lips.
We need not fear, though high the praise
  They pour on Zion's hill,
, Though the great name of David's son
  Their thoughts and stories fill.

Our sires were men of old renown,
  They conquered far and wide,
They reared on high their stately towers,
  Their palaces of pride;
But now we hear of one whose ships
  Sail on to east and west,
Where springs the sun in orient dawn,
  Where sinks he to his rest.

Our seers have gathered golden dust
  From out the sands of time,
With noble thoughts and music clear
  They sang their glorious chime;
But now men speak of one whose soul
  Is boundless as the sea,
Whose knowledge flows in one broad stream,
  Rejoicing, full, and free.

The Father of the sons of men,
    The God of Heaven most High,
We worshipped Him where mountain-peaks
    Soar upward to the sky ;
But lo ! they tell of one whose skill
    All realms of art explores,
Whose Temple opens for his God
    Its everlasting doors.

On, then, our heart is sick and faint,
    We weary with delay ;
We will not halt until we see
    That monarch's proud array ;
Then gazing, hearing, knowing all,
    Our soul at last will rest,
Or conquering in the noble strife,
    Or vanquished, self-confessed.

And then, if true this fame they bring
    Of wisdom wide and deep,
My secret thoughts in daylight clear,
    My visions when I sleep,
The vexing doubts that come and go,
    The cravings after light,
Will I, undaunted, though o'ercome,
    Lay bare before His sight.

'Twere worth all wanderings far and wide
   A king like this to know,
To let his speech, like choicest seed,
   Take root, and bud, and grow;
To sit and listen, day by day,
   To words of grace and truth,
To see his wisdom bright and clear
   In everlasting youth.

Then on, o'er desert, hill, and vale,
   Green pastures, stoniest plain,
With chariots, horses, camels, on,
   A queen's majestic train;
We stay not till our feet shall stand
   Within that golden shrine,
Until our eyes have seen the king
   In all his beauty shine.

II.

THE RETURN.

My father, yes, it was not false,
   That rumour from afar;
Above all mists and clouds it shines,
   That monarch's full-orbed star;

l saw his state with wondering eyes,
   I heard his words of grace,
I watched, half dumb with rapturous awe,
   The brightness of his face ;

The lofty brow, not swarth and dark,
   As Sheba's sons are seen,
But bright as comes the clear-eyed morn
   From out its cloudy screen ;
The eyes, now fierce with kingly wrath,
   Now soft as evening's glow,
The golden hair, whose clustering locks,
   Like waves of sunlight, flow.

As when a standard-bearer lifts
   His blazoned flag on high,
And chief among ten thousand stands,
   Beneath the orient sky,
So stood he, glorious as the sun,
   Arrayed in robes of gold;
And I, with wonder faint, confessed
   Not half the glory told.

Thou would'st not go, my father ; thou
   Did'st plead thy weight of years,
Death's shadow flung across thy path,
   Life's chances, age's fears ;

But I will tell thee all I heard
    Of that high wisdom's lore,
Till thou, from whom my soul learnt much,
    Shalt own I teach thee more.

Our ships went forth from Sheba's ports,
    They sailed up Edom's sea,
We passed the shores where Joktan's sons
    Roam wild, and fierce, and free ;
Where Elath's harbour opens wide,
    And then, in stately march,
Where Bozrah's rocks are crowned with towers,
    And spanned by loftiest arch.

We looked upon the accursèd sea,
    We breathed its sulphurous breath,
Where bleaching bones, and scurf of salt,
    Speak evermore of death ;
We crossed, where stately Jordan flows
    By many a grove of palm,
Where fragrant winds from Gilead bring
    Their gentle airs of balm.

Then up the vale whose rocks o'erhang
    The path of winter stream,
Until at last on wistful eyes
    The towers of Zion gleam ;

Where olives gray and hoar grow thick,
　We saw the vision bright;
The golden city, Home of Peace,
　Burst full upon our sight.

We saw the thousand bright-eyed youths
　In purple stiff with gold;
We saw the hosts of Israel march,
　Ten thousand warriors bold;
The chariot such as Pharaoh owns,
　The banners waving wide,
The throne where six proud lions stand
　As guards on either side.

But most where slopes the wide ascent
　To where Jehovah dwells,
Where still from choir of white-robed priests
　The Hallelujah swells;
Where, clad in purple robes from Tyre,
　He enters from the East,
The king, who walks in glorious state,
　Half-monarch, and half-priest.

We met; his eye glowed bright and free,
　I heard his speech distil,
Like wild bee's store of crystal gold,
　And heart and spirit fill;

He did not scorn my woman's thoughts,
　My passion's eager quest ;
His noblest words, his treasured lore,
　My spirit's cravings blest.

I asked, " O king, the nations bow
　To Gods on many a throne,
And many a name with song and dance
　As King and Lord they own ;
But which of all shall we adore
　As giving life and light,
What name may best His favour win,
　The Lord of boundless might ?"

He answered, " Lo ! the Lord is One,
　Above the heaven He dwells,
And day to night His power declares,
　And night to morning tells ;
Give Him thy heart : in truth and love
　Do thou His righteous will,
And He, thy Father, Lord of all,
　Shall all thy wish fulfil !"

I asked, " O king, the skies are drear,
　We wage a fruitless strife ;
The heart is faint, the hands hang down,
　We weary of our life ;

We toil in vain for wealth and fame,
   We gather and we waste ;
Yet fail to find the bread of life,
   The food the angels taste."

And he, " Who walks in light and truth,
   Shall find the fount of joy,
The peace which nought on earth can give,
   No power of man destroy ;
The child-like heart, the fear of God,
   Is truest wisdom found ;
And joy and goodness circle still
   In one unbroken round."

I asked, " O king ! the ways of God,
   They baffle and perplex ;
The evil prosper, nothing comes
   Their full-fed souls to vex ;
The righteous perish, crushed and scorned ;
   Their life in darkness ends ;
Is this the order and the truth
   Unerring counsel sends ?"

He answered, " Lo, thou see'st as yet ;
   The outskirts of His rule ;
He trains the child, He forms the man
   In suffering's varied school ;

Dire forms of evil hover still
　　Around the proud's success,
And thoughts of trust, and hope, and peace
　　The righteous mourner bless."

I asked, "Yet once again, O king,
　　This life, can it be all?
We toil and strive our little day,
　　And then the shadows fall;
Have we no goal to reach at last?
　　Has this wild sea no shore?
Has God no home where wearied souls
　　May rest for evermore?"

And he, "The things behind the veil
　　No mortal yet hath known;
On that far land the shadows rest
　　That shroud the Eternal Throne;
Yet this we know, in life or death,
　　His presence still is there;
And where that brightness fills the soul,
　　Is joy beyond compare."

So communed I, and every word
　　Went straight to heart and soul,
Dim thoughts made clear, and random will
　　Now striving for the goal;

I drank deep draughts of that clear fount,
    The well of life and truth,
As one new-born I went my way
    In gladness, as of youth.

And now the past is past; again
    On Sheba's coasts I dwell,
And never more my feet shall tread
    Where Jordan's flood-streams swell;
Yet still the days that then I knew
    Are worth long years to me,
And in the visions of the night
    That princely form I see.

That voice makes music in mine ear,
    And echoes in mine heart,
And thoughts steal in, with subtle power,
    And wonder-working art;
Of all that God has given of great,
    Or true, or pure, or fair,
The son of David stands supreme,
    And reigns unrivalled there.

God's image I have seen, unmarred
    By taint of evil will,
And in my heart's most sacred shrine
    That image lingers still;

It helps me, as I kneel and pray,
    To worthier thoughts of Him
Whom until now I have but known
    In vision dark and dim.

So glorious is the earthly type,
    God's beauty seen in man ;
And shall not God at last complete
    What thus His might began ?
How bright and wondrous when we know
    His power and love and grace,
And, leaving mists and clouds below,
    Look on Him face to face !

III.

TEN YEARS LATER.

And can it be?   Strange news they bring,
    These men from Edom's shore ;
A greater marvel meets us now
    Than that we heard before ;
The king who rose to glory's height,
    Whom but to see was bliss,
He falls, as none have fallen yet,
    In evil's dark abyss.

The son of David, God's beloved,
  Who spake in loftiest tone,
Of Him, whom, girt with seraphim,
  The highest heavens enthrone,—
His incense-smoke in Baal's shrine
  Floats, wreath-like, to the skies ;
He joins the wild and frenzied band
  Whose hymns to Baal rise.

He stands by Moloch's blazing pyre,
  . He hears the wailing cry ;
He sees the mother's blank despair,
  With cold and tearless eye ;
Where damsels gather, flushed with wine,
  He mingles, nothing loth,
And threads the whirling, dizzying dance
  In groves of Ashtaroth.

The eye has lost its wonted fire,
  The lips no longer smile ;
All spells of art and song are vain
  His deadness to beguile ;
For sated pride will leave its blank,
  And sated lust its sting,
And still the inexorable hours
  Their torturing penance bring.

The soul that looked through height and depth,
    And heavenly music heard,
And read, in sun, and moon, and stars,
    The Eternal Wisdom's word,
Now, plunged in magic's caverns dark,
    Seeks hidden spells and charms,
To bind the demons at his will,
    To shield his house from harms.

No more at earliest break of day
    He sits within the gate,
To hear from widows, orphans, poor,
    Their plaints against the great ;
The gardens fair with many a rose,
    The streamlets murmuring low,
These blind the eye, and stop the ear,
    To sights and sounds of woe.

The fine gold waxes dim ; so fades
    The vision from mine eyes ;
The idol, fallen from its shrine,
    Despised and broken lies ;
No more I see the form of God
    Imprinted on the seal ;
Those baleful eyes, those scoffing lips,
    God's foe, and man's, reveal.

Far nobler thou, in all thine age,
   Bent low with weight of years,
Dim-eyed and feeble, not without
   Sharp pain, and haunting fears ;
Thou still hast kept thy loyal soul,
   In steadfastness and truth,
And in thy heart of hearts there dwells
   The freshness of thy youth.

Far nobler he, of whom they tell,
   The man of Uz, who lay,
From head to foot one leprous sore,
   In anguish night and day ;
His spirit spake its cravings out,
   It yearned for Truth and Right ;
And so his wandering steps were led
   Through darkness into light.

The path to wisdom lies not there,
   By palace-gates and towers ;
The lowly hut, the wanderer's tent,
   The green field bright with flowers—
These teach their lessons day by day,
   They bid us still be calm,
And, through the weariness of life,
   Rings Nature's wondrous psalm.

F

I turn from all the varied state,
   Rich hues, devices rare,
The purple robes, the golden shields,
   The terraced garden fair ;
One pencilled flower excels them all,
   The lily shames the king ;
God clothes the hills in nobler gold,
   More radiant glows the spring.

Should'st Thou, O God, to man once more
   Give wisdom as the sea,
Should human voice in words divine
   In Thy name speak of Thee,
It were no child of lordly birth,
   No heir of kingly throne ;
The homeless, friendless, peasant-born,
   Thou claimest as Thine own.

No wreath of flowers encircles brows
   To gold and purple born,
Round temples bleeding, faint, and wan
   There twines the crown of thorn.
To Him I turn, that sufferer pale,
   In vision seen afar,
As turn the sages when they watch
   Their life's ascending star.

In that wide heart I find my home,
    That wisdom gives me light ;
There, sick and faint with love, I gaze
    Adoring, at the sight ;
To see great David's son enthroned
    Were worth a kingdom's loss,
But He, the Son of Man, shall reign
    O'er all men from His cross.

March 1863

MIRIAM OF MAGDALA.

———◆———

" Out of whom went seven devils."

WITH firm-pressed lips, and clenchèd hands she
    sat,
Her eyes now kindling with the fire of hell,
Now wildly vacant ; and with sudden burst,
As from a trance awakening, she would start,
And some loud chant, a strain of happier days,
Wild echoes of an ancient melody,
Would pass her pallid lips ; and oft she rent
The calm night air with fierce and fitful scream,
As one in anguish.   Then, for many days,
The trance returning, limbs as marble stiff,
The sense benumbed, she seemed as one half-dead ;
And not the warming clasp of mother's arm,
Nor the hot falling rain of mother's tears,
Nor childhood's sunny smile, nor laughing song
Could rouse her into life of womanhood.
Her hair that once hung down in raven folds,

O'er marble brow, in crispèd, wavy curls,
While golden circlet shone upon its dark,
An aureole of brightness, and men said,
In very love of beauty, as she passed,
" Behold, our Miriam with the braided locks !"—
That hair now swept in wild disorder down,
And never touch of woman's loving hand
Brought back the old array, but fingers fierce
Tore through it, flung it to the ruthless winds
In sore despair, as though the burning heat
Of brow and brain had made intolerable
That veil of woman's glory.
                                    How it came
Men knew not.   Not for her had been the strife
With adverse fortune, and the world's rough blasts
Had spared her.   Heiress of her father's house,
She dwelt at ease, and in the city's street
Her home rose high, and spread its courtyard wide,
Where pleasant fountains murmured in the shade,
And clustering vine hung purpling on the wall,
And rose of Sharon shed its rich perfume,
And fair pomegranates bore their ruby gems
Deep set in emerald brightness.   Many friends
Were hers, the elders of the house of God,
The Rabbis, and the Levites, and the Priests,
And sang her praise.   Nor had she known the shame
Of those who cast the pearl of life away
For swine to tread on.   Never lip of scorn

Had breathed her name in mocker's scurril jest,
Nor slanderer's whisper touched her fair repute
Of maiden pureness.   Clad in chastity,
Her soul was white from all the stain of sense,
Her bosom heaved not with the sighs of love ;
And youth that wooed with eager ecstasy,
And age that lavished gifts of gold and gems,
Won the same answer, " They were nought to her."
    And so the years went on ; and then there came
A dull gray blight upon the roseate dawn,
And all the flowers, the fair, fresh flowers of youth,
Were withered, and the joy of life was gone.
First, wayward answers, petulant reproach,
The smartings of a soul that knows not peace,
The sense of some vast gulf, that, opening wide,
Had given a vision of the central void,
And nether fires that burn perpetually,
While she, half spell-bound, half in apathy,
Was borne along, she knew not where or how,
In one great terror.   Night that comes to all,
And brings soft influence from the angel sleep
To quicken weary souls to stronger life,
Brought none to her. The long, long hours passed by,
And still her eyes glared on with fitful flash ;
And spectral horrors of earth's monstrous growths,
Dim forms gigantic of the ghastly dead,
These moved before her, now in slow array,
And now in quickest onset, like the rush

Of armies to the battle, and the sun
Looked in upon that vigil of affright,
And found her waking still, her every nerve
Wrought to the pitch of keenest agony,
Not weeping, (that refreshment of the soul
Had not been granted,) but with moans and shrieks
Making the air re-echo.   So she loathed
Her life, and men shrank from her in their fear ;
" Lo ! Miriam with the braided locks is mad ;
Seven demons hold her."
                          And ere long one came
From Gadara, who through all Gennesareth's coasts
Had made men quail, and women· shriek and shrink ;
Naked, and foul, and frenzied,—in the tombs,
The dwelling-place of foul and festering death,
He chose his home, and, howling in despair,
Rending the air with curses, hating men
His brothers, hating God, his Father, more,
He burst his chains, as he of Zorah tore
Of old the green withs of the Philistines,
And smote down those that bound him.   Thus for
        years.
His life had passed, but now with altered mien,
Clothed, and in calmness came he, telling all
Of ONE who freed him from that thraldom vile,
And bade his legion-foes depart, and vex
His soul no longer.   And he felt them go ;
The war was over, and the peace was come,

No more two voices spoke within his heart,
Two promptings tore the miserable life,
One bidding curse and hate, blaspheme and die,
And one that craved for kindly look of love,
Friend's touch, and brother's help. The spell was gone,
And all the soul went forth towards its Lord,
And fain had kept that pitying glance in sight,
And gained the guidance of that steadfast hand,
And with Him journeyed over hill and lake.
It might not be.   The soul so long convulsed,
Still heaving with the earthquake and the storm,
Had need of rest, had need of earthly friends,
To knit once more the broken threads of life ;
And o'er the parched and howling wilderness
Must fall the dew of daily charities,
Till once again the soft green grass should spring,
And gladden in the shining after rain.
And so among the people of his home
He came and dwelt, and told the wondrous tale,
And then the marvel spread.   From Gerasa,
Through Dalmanutha, yea, through all the coasts
Where boats of fishers plied from beach to beach,
From green Bethsaida to Capernaum's bay,
It came at last to Magdala.   They sent
To ask the Healer, and the Healer came ;
No Rabbi with his spells of mystic sound,
No wandering charmer, skilled in ancient lore,
Egypt's dark rites, or seal of Solomon,

But One whose pure and perfect sinlessness
Drew with the power of wondrous sympathy
All goodness to itself, gave life to germs
Long buried deep below the sand of years,
Poured in the oil that fed the slumbering flame,
Bound up the reed the world had harshly bruised,
And gave the captive freedom.   So He came,
And Miriam heard the word that bade her live,
Break from her fetters, trample on the thoughts,
Half demon-like, half-brutal, that had kept
Her soul in thraldom ; and, the dark hour past,
She rose to higher life, serener thoughts.
She, too, would follow where the Master led,
Up the steep hill, or on the dusty way,
In scorching heat, or winter's evening chill,
Her life's one thought to give Him of His own,
The true thank-offering of a life restored
To Him, the great Restorer.

                  So they went,
That band of sisters.   One had lived in courts,
Had seen the Tetrarch's proud magnificence,
Had heard the summons of the Baptist's voice
Strike terror and amazement ; one had dwelt
(Salome, mother of the fiery ones,
The sons of thunder) by Gennesareth's shore ;
And each her story had to tell of love,
And might, and pity, from the Lord of life,
The Healer of the body and the soul ;

And Miriam joined that goodly company,
Her heart being one with theirs.   At early morn,
Erc yet the dew had risen in fragrant steam,
They rose from slumber, prayed, and journeyed forth,
Still keeping in the rear, while vanward marched
The Master and His followers.   Should it chance
He stopped to speak to all the wondering crowd,
And preach the tidings of good news from God,
Then they, in meekest reverence, lingered round
The utmost margin of the encircling throng,
And heard rejoicing.   When the day was done,
They onward sped to nearest village-town,
Prepared the chamber, spread the simple meal,
And washed the feet that all day long had toiled
O'er the hot pathway, through the scorching dust.
And soon the number grew.   There came to them
Full many a Galilean maid or wife,
Owning or son or brother in the Twelve,
Now pressing on to keep the Paschal feast,
And wait the Kingdom's glory.   She was there,
Round whom there lingered yet the virgin's grace,
The mother's chastened meekness ; and to her,
As namesake, helper, friend, the Magdalene
Turned with the love that worships.   Many years
Might lie between them ; one was worn and gray,
With grief yet more than age, and one still fair
In all the prime of full-grown womanhood ;
And yet each loved the other : both were joined

In the strong band of all-absorbing love
For One above them both.   As daughter true,
With loving mother, so they journeyed forth,
And still at morn and eve they prayed their prayer,
Or stood behind the carvèd lattice-work,
At Sabbath morn in village synagogue,
With hearts that beat together, and they found
The self-same helper.   He, whom most of all
The Master loved, Jochanan, from the heights
Of green Bethsaida, by Gennesareth,
Was truest friend to both, would bring them word
How best to journey, how escape the throng
Of gathering foes, how keep their tranquil life
In midst of all confusion.   And to him
They gave a mother's and a sister's love ;
Rejoiced in soul when he, at even-tide,
The day's work done, would tell them golden words
Fresh dropt from holiest lips—the mystic speech
Of parables and proverbs, priceless pearls,
For which the seekers had to search full hard,
And plunge in deepest waters—these he brought,
That they might share his joy, when truths of God,
Long hidden, from behind the veil shone forth,
The orient dawning of the perfect day.
Glad welcome had they from the sisters twain,
(Another Miriam one,) whom Bethany
Beheld with wonder, whom the Master loved,
Whose brother, Eleazar, He had raised

From out his four days' sleep.   Nor did there fail
That sister band far other fellowship ;
One came among them, bowed with foulest shame,
Who, in the dark, wide places of the streets
Had walked with face unveiled and pencilled brows ;
But she, too, loved the Teacher who had shown
Divinest pity, manliest tenderness,
And lavishing the heaped-up gains of years,
The wages of the sin that now she loathed,
On costliest unguent in its crystal vase,
She poured it out upon the Lord's dear feet,
While thickly fell the shower of blinding tears,
And golden hair, down dropping like a cloud,
Veiled her in sunlight from the eyes of scorn.
Much had she sinned, much also had she loved,
And Miriam's heart clave to her, pitying
The shame she had not known.   Of all the band
No two were closer bound in sisterhood
Than they, the sinner and the Magdalene.
    So went they day by day, as darker grew
The storms around their Master, till at last
They joined the throng of that great Paschal-tide,
Crossed from the East, and o'er the gleaming ford,
Where Jordan flows by many a feathery grove,
Came to the town of palm-trees, toiled along
The hot steep road to where the pathway climbs
The eastern slope of hoary Olivet,
And rested in Bethania.   Then a feast,

A gathering of the poor, the maimed, the halt,
The pilgrim and the stranger ; once again
The fragrant breaking of the spikenard vase,
(That Miriam hearing from the friends who came,
Of what the sinner did in Simon's house,)
And then the morn broke brightly.   So they went,
Disciples, people, all, a glorious train,
And He, the Master, rode, a Prince of Peace,
In kingly state towards Jerusalem.
No battle of confusèd noise was there,
Nor garments rolled in blood · no chariot bore
The conquering hero through the heaps of slain,
But loud hosannas rent the noon-tide air,
And costly garments hid the whitening dust,
And waving branches of the fresh green palm
Smote off the summer-flies, or, cast to earth,
Made a bright path for that triumphant tread.
They saw it in the distance, all the band
Of those true sisters, and their women's hearts
Leapt up for joy, for now they deemed the hour,
Long waited for, had come, and Israel's hopes
Had gained their high fulfilment.   Now the King
(So dreamt the Maiden-mother of her son,
Not knowing that the sword was near her heart)
Would claim the glory of His father's throne,
Feed with full hand the hungry and the poor,
And send the rich back empty.   And the twain,
The sinner and the Magdalene, they joyed

To think that they should as His handmaids serve,
Where gilded columns rise from cedarn floors
In Zion's loftiest palace.

      Soon the dream
Was past, and lo ! the conquest had not come ;
And they as women, keeping to the house,
But little knew. They heard of gathering crowds
That filled the gates of all the Temple's courts ;
And whispers ran, the priests in secret met
Had planned His death, yet fain must wait awhile,
In very fear of that great multitude
Who held Him as a prophet. So the days
Ran on ; the holy Paschal feast was o'er,
And on the morn that followed, ere the sun
Looked down upon the fig-tree and the vine,
They heard the rumour, "Lo ! the deed is done ;
Among the Twelve was one a traitor found,
And all the rest forsook Him." Then there came
The hasty Court, the sentence, and the scourge,
The mockery, and, ere yet the noontide heat
Had come, the sad, slow march to Golgotha.
And as He passed, they wept Him and bewailed,
They, and those daughters of Jerusalem,
Who counted Israel's consolation near,
And now found shame and darkness. And He looked
In pity on them, bade them weep no more
For Him, but for themselves, their children dear,
The city which their hearts exulted in.

"If they, our conquerors, on the green tree wreak
Such vengeance; if the blameless Prophet bear
This cross, what depth of suffering fathomless
Shall come upon my people, when the tree,
Barren, and dry, and withered, to the axe .
Shall yield itself a victim!" Then a pause,
A gathering gloom, and then from out the crowd
They slipped, and followed where the crosses stood,
The mourning mother and the Magdalene;
And with them that disciple whom He loved, ˙
Whose face, well-known to all the priestly throng,
Won silent pity, and a shelter gave
Against all scorn and outrage. So they went,
And stood, and spake not, hand close clasped in hand,
Noting each pulse of quivering agony,
Catching each word that dropped from parchèd lips,
Till all was over. Then they turned away,
Watched the pale form laid gently in the tomb;
And ere the sun had crimsoned all the west,
And Sabbath stillness fell upon the streets,
They bought their spices. Now her time was come;
First one and then another, in His life,
Had bought their unguents, precious as the oil
Which poured down Aaron's ephod to his skirts,
With kingly perfume, and on head and feet
Had lavished all; but now when life was gone,
When never more should glance of His wake up
The soul within her, nor His gentle voice,

Like soft, sweet music, fall upon her heart,
When neither hope of favour nor of praise—
The praise of men beholding her great love,
The praise of Him on whom the love was spent—
Could enter in, but love, and love alone,
The one strong master-passion of her soul,
Sway all the tides of being,—now she too
Would do her service, pour the liquid nard
Upon the dead, cold limbs, and wrap them round
In precious spice, and Egypt's finest lawn.
And so they rested, she and that true band
Of chosen sisters, all the Sabbath-day,
And, half for fear, and half for woe, stirred not
From out that upper chamber, where they dwelt,
To temple-service at the hour of prayer,
Where in the women's court, the anthems rise
Clear, high, and full, and mingle with the chants
Of priests and Levites ; nor, behind the screen,
Stood up to pray where Galileans met
In that, the pilgrims' synagogue ; but still
From morn to eve they sat, and wept, and prayed,
As widowed mother weeping for her son,
As sisters who lament a brother lost,
As true disciples mourning for their Lord.
And Miriam; most of all, plunged deep in woe,
As though all waves and storms swept over her,
With brows close knit, and tight-clenched lips sat there,
O'er one thought brooding, that her Lord was gone,

On one hope feeding, that her hands should give
That Lord a kingly burial   So they sat,
Until the moon was shining in the East,
And Sabbath rest was ended ; and they drank,
As mourners drink at funerals of the dead,
One cup of wine in memory of their Lord,
And ate their bread, half-choked with stifled sobs ;
And then through all the hours of eventide
They toiled, and waited till the East was gray,
And roseate flush upon the furthest cloud
Proclaimed the day had risen.   Then they went,
(Not all, for she, the mourning mother, stayed,
In silent sorrow, not unmixed with hope,)
And Miriam with them, where in Joseph's tomb
Their Lord was laid.   Through streets that still were
      dumb,
No feet yet stirring, to the northern gate,
Through terraced garden, where the air was cool
With plashing fountains, and the breath of flowers
Was fresh and sweet, as was the breeze of old
In Eden's groves ; and then before the tomb
They stood, where, hollowed in the fresh-hewn rock,
The cave oped wide its mouth.   And lo ! the stone,
Of which their hearts had nourished anxious fears,
So far beyond their woman's strength to move.
Was rolled aside.   The keepers all were fled,
The grave was empty, grave-clothes laid aside,
And two bright forms, arrayed in garments white,

G

Like those young priests who in the Temple courts
Wave incense, sat within, and spake to them ;
"Why seek ye here the living with the dead ?
Your Lord is risen."   Others heard the words,
And ran for joy, full-flushed and eager joy,
To tell their friends and brothers.   But for her,
For Miriam, who through all the weary night
Had kept her watch, was neither joy nor faith ;
She stood as one bewildered, let them pass,
Her friends and sisters, lingered there alone,
Her eyes still fixed upon the emptied cave ;
And all the glory of those heavenly ones,
That vision of the angels, seemed a dream
That vanishes on waking.   "Could this be
And was she robbed of love's last ministry,
The homage upon which her heart was set,
The all that still was left her in her life ?"
(And so, as though a gap were opening wide
Beneath her feet in darkness of the night,
And once again she trembled o'er the pit,)
She stood as in the woe of former days,
In blank amazement ; and her only speech
Was this, that He, her dearest Lord, was gone,
And where He was she knew not ; and the sky
Of life was dark, and yet a little while,
And all the madness, all the fierce despair,
Had come on her once more ; when lo ! a voice,
"Why weepest thou, O woman ?" and she turned,

Just waking from her trance, with eager quest,
And spoke the passionate craving of her heart :
" My Lord is gone. Ah, sir ! and can'st thou tell
Where they have laid Him ?" And the answer came
In voice as clear and pitying, yet as strong
As when, of old, it broke the demon's spell,
And in her home, in pleasant Magdala,
Had called her by her name. And then once more
The spell was broken. Now the veil was rent
Which kept her from the knowledge of her Lord ;
And with one cry, loud, eager, passionate,
" Rabboni, O my Master !" falling down
In love adoring, to that Master's feet
She clung in rapture. Yet it might not last,
That high-wrought mood of purest ecstasy ;
That touch had something of impassioned fear,
Had something of the love that cleaves to earth ;
And souls that seek for converse with their Lord
Must calmer grow, and breathe in gentler strain
The softer music of a soul at peace ;
Must still endure, although the skies be dark,
As seeing, through the shadows of the night,
His glory who remains invisible.
And so still pitying, still with gentlest words,
He put her from him, bade her hear and tell,
That, though He tarried yet a little while,
The time was short, and then His hour would come,
When He, raised high above the heaven of stars,

Should show Himself no more ; and then her love
Might cling in rapture to the Eternal Arm,
Might prostrate lie before His feet who walks
Upon the mighty waters.   Now her task
Must be to spread the tidings of great joy,
Proclaiming " Christ is risen."

                        So she went ;
And more we know not.   Seen a few short hours
In clearest sunlight, then in shadow deep
Her life passed on.   But this at least we know,
That He who loved loves even to the end,
And she had learnt the lesson that He taught ;
And when with earthly eyes she gazed no more,
She saw, as though the heavens were opened wide,
And knew Him present, when with two or three
She prayed, or sang His praises ; felt Him near,
When on the sick she poured the healing oil,
Or washed the feet of pilgrims.   So she lived,
Still joined in bands of closest sisterhood ;
And when at last life's little span was o'er,
Or in the graves that border Kedron's vale,
Or by the walls of ancient Magdala,
Or on far shores beyond the glittering sea,
They laid her to her rest, and o'er her tomb,
Graved on the rock, they wrote, " She sleeps at peace."

     June 1865.

DEMODOCOS.

———◆———

τὸν πέρι Μοῦσ' ἐφίλησε, δίδου δ' ἀγαθόν τε κακόν τε·
ὀφθαλμῶν μὲν ἄμερσε, δίδου δ' ἡδεῖαν ἀοιδήν.

> "Him the Muse greatly loved, and gave to him
> Both good and evil, of his eyes bereaved,
> And gave him sweetest song."

I.

NOT in thy wrath, O Goddess, not in wrath,
    Thy hand was on me laid,
That thus I tread my dark and lonely path,
    In ever deepening shade ;

Time was I revelled, in my youth's full glee,
    In dances all the night ;
And when the dawn was on the eastern sea,
    Climbed up the mountain height.

The robber wolf we chased with hound and spear,
    Or, on the hill-side's slope,

Caught in our toils the stately antlered deer,
    Or bright-eyed antelope :

Across the bays I steered my dancing boat,
    Among the purple isles,
Where far and wide the sparkling waters float
    In twice ten thousand smiles ;

And when the grapes hung purple on the vine,
    I joined the vintage train ;
Or went with reapers, from Demêter's shrine,
    To store the golden grain :

And, hot and panting when the work was done,
    Plunged in the cool, dark stream ;
And, where the plane-tree tempers summer's sun,
    Lay down to doze and dream.

And one there was, the partner of my life,
    The idol of my heart,
Who, bearing now the nobler name of wife,
    Is mine till death shall part :

With ardent gaze we read each other's eyes,
    And scanned the secret deep,
Where in each soul the hidden fountain lies
    Of love that cannot sleep.

And oh ! my children's faces, they were dear,
    The wistful eye's delight ;
Or beaming gladly, or with childhood's tear,
    Yet still abiding bright ;—

All this I knew ; all this is vanished now,
    I see no more the day ;
The Gods have done it, and I needs must bow :
    They gave ; They take away.

II.

That loss was great.   I could not hide
    The bitter pang it brought at first,
The strange new forms of life untried,
    The fear that bad might pass to worst ;

To grope my way in midnight gloom,
    To need the touch of guiding hand :—
I fain had rested in the tomb,
    And seen the glass run out its sand.

And yet the days that came and went,
    Brought airs of balm with power to heal ;
And lo ! I read the pure intent
    That smote me, but to make me feel

How nobler far the light that streams
  Within, upon the yearning soul,
Than aught I saw in brightest gleams
  Of stars that circle round the pole.

Then all the ceaseless tide of sense
  Flowed on in one o'ermastering flood;
I could not search or scan, and hence
  I took the evil with the good:

The pulse of joy in all my veins
  Ran riot, but the soul was dumb;
I counted not or loss or gains,
  I let the moments go and come;

The bursting fulness of delight
  Left room for neither words nor song,
And summer's day and winter's night,
  Like one broad river, flowed along.

I lived my life, and yet I lacked
  The power to look behind the veil,
The vision of the central fact
  Which lasts when all besides shall fail.

Was this true life, which did not know
  The meaning of its grief or joy?

Where then were all the thoughts that grow,
  And make the man surpass the boy?

III.

But now Thy hand, dear Muse, hath swept the strings,
  And drawn forth notes of wondrous melody;
And, like the bird that through the dark night sings,
  My soul in darkness yields itself to Thee.

The visions of old days are with me still,
  The golden sunsets, and the purple isles,
The clear, brown sparkling of the mountain rill,
  Fair face, bright eyes, sweet flowers, and children's
    smiles;

And lo! from out the story of the past,
  The forms of heroes throng in dread array,
The ancient rivers sweeping strong and fast,
  The tower-crowned cities that have had their day;

Through gates of Thebes, 'mid clouds of glittering dust,
  Lo! the proud chariots and the horsemen pass;
And Troy, though buried in the graves of lust,
  Still rears on high her battlements of brass;

Achilles sits upon the lonely shore,
   And Hector's helmet flashes in the sun,
And Argive Helen, fairer than before,
   Warms the cold hearts whose race is all but run ;

Gray Nestor drops his honeyed words and wise,
   And young Patroclos falls before his prime,
And calm Andromache, with steadfast eyes,
   Loves with a love that faileth not with time :

I see them all by fair Scamandros' stream,
   Fighting and feasting, toiling, taking rest ;
The pageant flits before me as a dream ;
   And yet it makes my life.   What is, is best :

I would not change the world where now I live,
   In which I dwell as Maker, Lord, and King,
For all that youth, power, beauty, sight could give,
   Man's wisdom, lion's strength, or eagle's wing.

Thou, Muse, art kind, and gentle is Thy smile,
   Thy music charms the wayward heart's mistrust ;
I will not doubt it, but will wait awhile,
   Till all is ended.   Lo ! the Gods are just.

IV.

Yes, I must wait.   The veil
Of mist and cloud surrounds the distant land ;
　　The poets tell their tale,
And yet the darkness lies on either hand ;

　　I fain would upward rise,
And see the Gods on each Olympian hill,
　　Where throned above the skies,
The glory of their presence lingereth still ;

　　Where Zeus, the Thunderer, reigns,
And king Apollo walks, in light arrayed ;
　　Or, darting o'er the plains,
Swift Hermes glides through many a moss-grown glade.

　　But ah ! the eyes are dim,
The feet are weak that fain would upward move ;
　　I cannot speak of Him,
Whom yet I faintly feel, and feebly love.

　　Those tales of ancient days
That charmed my youth, I sing them o'er and o'er ;
　　Men love to hear my lays,
And so the story waxes evermore.

But lo ! from first to last,
The heart yet feels the void that nought can fill ;
Through all that fabled past,
No fountain flows our burning thirst to still ;

The Gods in all their might
Are feebler far than heroes we have known ;
No glory infinite,
Surrounds their brow, or hovers o'er their throne :

But still in hot debate,
They strive and wrangle like the sons of men ;
And jealousy and hate
Turn high Olympos to a robber's den.

I sing of Hera's ire,
And tell the tale of Aphrodite's sin,
Prometheus' stolen fire,
The Titans' struggle, thrones in Heaven to win.

They still will have it so,
These good Phæacians, when the mirth is free ;
And yet too well I know
All these my songs, O God, unworthy Thee.

V.

I feel the void, and yet the days are sweet,
   And sunny is the evening of my life ;
   The months glide on, and never voice of strife
Mars the soft music where the waters meet :

They lead me through each dell and flowery glade,
   Where great Alcinoös spreads his garden fair ;
   And there I breathe the cool and balmy air,
And odorous shrubs give perfume in the shade ;

Or, when the sun falls hot upon my head,
   These sightless eyeballs feel the touch of light,
   A crimson dawn breaks in upon the night,
And speaks of life uprising from the dead.

My children's children clasp my knees, and I,
   Pass lightest fingers o'er each fair, young face,
   And all but see the beauty and the grace
That glows through brow, fair cheek, and beaming eye ;

And where in groves the sculptured Goddess stands,
   In cool, smooth marble in her leafy shrine,
   Round each fair limb my garlands I entwine,
And own her beauty with adoring hands.

And when at eve the king and princes meet,
  And in his palace hold high festival,
  To strike the harp that guides the dancers' feet
For me, for me, the blind old man, they call.

They give me wine from out the cups of gold,
  And through my veins the warmer pulses steal;
  The Muses then their hidden might reveal,
And bring once more the scenes and days of old.

Admiring murmurs pass from guest to guest,
  And, when I cease, burst out in loud acclaim ;
  They crown my brows with laurel, and my name
They rank among their noblest and their best.

And once there came a stranger to our shores,
  Who many seas and many lands had crossed,
  And now, a wanderer, lonely, tempest-tossed,
Sat listening to the songs and deeds of yore ;

Though bold and strong was he, unused to weep,
  Yet did my song of joys, and hopes, and fears
  That once were his, move all his soul to tears ;
My voice broke up the fountains of the deep :

For he had fought at Troy, had known them all,
  Achilles, Aias, Hector, and the rest

Who wander now, in isles of amaranth blest ;
His eyes beheld their greatness and their fall ;

Oh ! noblest height of all a minstrel's prayer,
   When hearts of heroes own the mighty spell,
   And through their soul the tides of passion swell,
And their lips echo each melodious air.

He heeds not then the praise or blame of kings ;
   Blindness, and grief, and age are nought to him ;
   Though strength be feeble, and though eyes be dim,
He soars on high, before the Gods he sings.

They hear his voice, and They approve his song,
   They shed their glory on his lonely path ;
   No, Muse, Thou did'st not smite me in thy wrath,
Thy love has watched and guided all along.

My harp's last notes shall echo to Thy praise ;
   My heart's last thoughts shall be of thanks and joy ;
   The blind old man is happier than the boy,
And truth and mercy follow all my days.

   April 1865.

CLAUDIA AND PUDENS.

COME, friends, where I shall lead you.   Follow on
  To where, o'er tangled briar and sandy heap,
Yon cypress waves its head ; and there, half-hid
In all the wild confusion of the place,
An entrance arched, and hollowed in the rock,
Shall meet your eyes.   Fear not the dim, dark gloom
That makes a midnight while the noontide sun
Floods all above with fire.   The shadows soon
Will grow familiar.   Through the mazy tracks
Your feet will wander, threading out your way
To cave and cell, a labyrinth of rock ;
And there, while overhead the city's stir,
Like sullen murmurs of a distant sea,
Floats evermore, for you is refuge safe.
No bloodhound's bay shall hunt you to the death,
Nor hungry Greekling play the informer's part,
Eaves-dropping at your converse.   I have known
Worse times than these, when loud the cry was heard,
" The Christians to the lions," and the flames

Glared horribly, as torches meet for hell,
Where Nero's gardens spread their terraced walks,
And murmuring fountains mingled with the cry
Of sharpest torment ; yet we shelter found
Beneath the shadow of the caves and rocks,
Beneath the shadow of the wings of God,
Until the tyrant's storms were overpast ;
And so shall ye find refuge.   Morn and eve,
In secret gathering, where the flickering lamp
Gleams redly through the darkness, prayer and hymn
Our true hearts offer to our Shepherd true,
For those that live, and those that sleep in Him ;
We break the bread and drink the wine of God,
And so our lone, dark catacomb becomes
The great King's banquet-hall, and we, His guests,
Are sharers in His kingdom.   Onward then,
And, when the sun is crimson in the west,
Meet me once more in peace.   Till then, farewell.

.   .   .   .   .   .

'Tis well : I see you, and I count you up,
As shepherd counts his gathered flock at night,
In fear lest wolf have seized his wandering sheep,
And, should one fail, goes forth upon the hills
To seek and save the lost one.   Now, thank God,
Not one is wanting.   Neither through the maze
Of these rough chambers, nor in crowded lanes,
The dens of shame and guilt, beyond the bridge
Which spans the widening Tiber, need I roam

II

In that sore quest.   I see and know you all ;
I know your tales of suffering and of crime :
Thou hast looked on and seen thy master burn,
And stretched no hand to help him, breathed no prayer
To soothe him in his anguish :—thou, though young,
Art stained with evil.   Here I see the brow
Still bright with guileless truth ; and there the cross
Speaks of Christ's faithful soldier.   Scars of scourge,
Half healed, proclaim the slave's hard punishment ;
And Roman matron, stripped of ring and robe,
Tells of the husband's power to curse and wrong,
Forgiving every crime of sense or soul,
The harlot's life, the wild imperious speech,
All but the one offence unpardonable,
The sin of being a Christian.   So it is ;
And, penitent or steadfast, ye are met,
Like those of old, in dens and caves of earth,
And bear your witness to an evil world
Of Him who is to conquer.   He will give
His peace to those that seek it.   Praise His name,
Praise Him for this sure refuge, praise yet more
For all our brothers who at last have won
The martyr's crown, and 'neath the altar rest,
And cry, " How long, O Lord ? " and blend their
        prayers   .
With incense-wreaths that float toward the throne,
And, robed in white, and bearing branch of palm,
Go forth to meet the Monarch on His path,

In statelier march than that on Olivet,
When He, the Prince of Peace, His people sought,
And they received Him not.   And ye shall hear,
Now that their course is ended, what till now
Was kept in darkness.   For a while forget
Your separate sorrows, all your selfish griefs,
And listen while I tell you what I know
Of Claudia and of Pudens.

      Many springs
Have gladdened earth, and many winters bound
The streams in fetters, since the early youth
When first I saw them.   I, whom now ye know,
Your elder, and the bishop of your souls,
Eubulus, then in boyhood grew, a slave
Sold in the market, bought, and sold again,
Till, so God willed it, Pudens made me his,
And I in that new service found new life.
Young was he then, the pride of all the youth,
The glory of the wrestling-ground and schools ;
No feet more swift to race the Circus round,
No arms more strong to stem the swollen stream
Of Tiber in the spring-tide : so he lived,
Wealthy, of noble lineage, genial too,
With kindly smile rewarding willing toil,
And ruling, not as others rule, by fear
Of brand or scourging, but by gentlest law
Of noblest nature.   True, the taint was there,
The taint which clung to all our older life :

He laughed, and sang, and revelled with the rest,
Half shrinking from the foulness, half enthralled
(As sailors venturing near the Siren's shores
Hear the sweet song, and lose their power to steer)
By the bright sparkling of the flashing wit,
The ever-ready answer.   Even there,
In that putrescent slime of forms unclean,
There gleamed a phosphor-lustre, and it hid
The naked shame.   And so he lived his youth,
A soldier in the high Prætorian band
That guards the Emperor's safety ; and ere long
There came a prisoner, sent by Festus here,
(Ye know his name ; give thanks for all he did,
And pray that he may find his rest in Christ,)
Paul, born in Tarsus, and our Pudens chanced,
From soldiers who had watched the prisoner well,
Fast bound to him with chains, to hear the tale
Of all that wondrous life.   'Twere long to tell
The story of the magic of his speech,
The words that went like arrows to their mark,
The subtle tact, the mystic ecstasy,
The playful humour, not one whit behind
Our Martial or Catullus ; dauntless soul,
Meekness unfeigned, and wondrous charity ;
With prætors and centurions bold to claim
His utmost right, and with the humblest slave
Conversing as an equal, so he came,
A marvel and a mystery.   Pudens heard,

Went, saw, was conquered.   Then there came the
    change,
The strivings of a life of nobler aims,
New hopes, and wider thoughts.   Half breaking off,
Half letting fall the old companionships,
He turned from those gay revellers of the past,
To join the pale young Jew who came with Paul,
Reserved and thoughtful, shunning feast and dance,
In lonely walks on yonder Alban hills,
Or, where his race across the Tiber dwell,
Went with him to the chamber where they met
To eat, and worship God.   And me he taught
What thus he learnt, yea, told me all the tale
Of Him who died on Golgotha, and rose
Lord of the dead and living.   Slave no more,
I served him as a brother, rendering back
All former kindness, counting all I did
As done to ONE in whom we both were free.
His former friends looked on and smiled, and
    shrugged
Their shoulders with the scorn of men who know
Mankind in all their weakness.   "Lo! one more
Is added to the dreamers of the world,
Who fain would turn the old earth upside down :
These fancies of the new philosophy,
Whose founder, scorned and hated by his own,
Died as a brigand dies, will run their course,
Turn some few weak ones mad, like this our friend,

And then die out. 'Twere well imperial Rome
Should crush it down at once."

       So spake they then ;
And Martial, he made merry with it all,
Called me Eucolpus, bosom friend and true,
Instead of trusty slave ; and once, when I,
(Pudens being smitten with the fever's touch,)
In new-born zeal of anxious faith and fear,
Took on my head the Nazarite's holiness,
He with glib tongue, and ready thought of ill,
Made sport of me, as though I still had lived
As others lived, and to Apollo made
My offering of the golden locks of youth.
But Claudia . . . . lo ! I linger on my way,
And tell you not of her who needs must be
The centre of my story.

       Fair she was
With all her nation's beauty, (for she came
From far Britannia, where the Ocean girds
Its last and wildest islands,) and her blood
Flowed from the veins of King Cogidobun,
Barbarian monarch wearing crown of gold,
And amber armlets wreathed with rows of pearls,
Whom Pudens once had known when Claudius sent
His legion to the Regni. Courteous guest
Found kindly host ; and thus, through all the change
Of time and fortune, still the king was firm
In friendship to the Romans, wavering not

When others fell away in open fight,
Or mined and countermined in secret plot;
And so our Pudens helped to build a shrine
For Neptune and Minerva; and the King,
To that barbaric name we scarce can speak
Joined that which Cæsar bore, full cheap reward,
Which yet he prized above all gold or gems,
As craving for a fellowship with us,
The world's great rulers.   So his infant child
Grew up as Claudia, very fair to see,
Eyes of clear azure, as the sapphire shines
In softest moonlight, brow of loveliest hue,
Not simply pale, as sculptured marble past
Beyond its first true whiteness to the tint
That speaks of coming age, nor such as oft
Our Roman matrons boast of through the tricks
And craft of art, but white as I have seen
The snow-crowned Alps, when morning's earliest sun
Has flushed them with the beauty of the rose;
And over brow and shoulder flowed the stream
Of silken hair, a very shower of gold,
While face and form both told of maiden grace,
Fresh as the dawn, and free as mountain breeze,
Still guarded in the purity of home,
Where those her Northern kinsmen kept aloof
From Rome's contagion.   And in this her prime,
Half hostage and half friend, she came to us
Beneath Pomponia's care.   On Britain's shore

The two had met, Pomponia, worn and sad,
With life's strange chances, weary of the world,
Sick of its shadows, craving for repose;
And Claudia, with the world as yet untried,
Her heart as yet untainted.   And their souls
Clave each to each, as mother to a child,
And child to mother; and the matron brought
The maid of Britain, hardly yet sixteen,
To this imperial city.   Strange its ways,
And half bewildering to her.   In her fear
She shrank into herself, while Roman dames
Looked on her in their scorn; nor could she bear
Her part with them in all the show and pomp,
Nor wear their filmy vestments, nor look on
While Gauls and Britons stained the sand with blood,
Saluting Cæsar as they marched to death,
And wrestled with the panthers.   So she grew,
As grows a lily in its veil of green,
Fragrant and pure, while all around it soar
Tall poppies flaunting in their scarlet robes,
Or crimson roses, flushed and overblown,
Meet wreath for drunkard's revelling; and ere long
Fresh dew from heaven on that fair lily fell,
And gave it holier beauty.   Still she turned,
Pomponia, weary of the shows of life,
To those who told of peace and joy beyond;
And so it chanced there came across her path,
Our Phœbe and Priscilla, and from them

She heard of that same Teacher of the East,
Our Lord and Master, heard how He had come
To save the wanderers, heard His words of love,
"All ye that labour, weary ones and sad,
Come ye to me, and I will give you rest,"
And hailed them as a message sent to her,
For she was weary, and she craved for rest.
And thus they too half joined our little band,
Forsook the fashion and the pride of life,
And men reproached them for their altered life,
Their gloom and strictness.

                  So they met once more
Pudens and Claudia, who, in earlier days,
Had met in Britain, and his heart was drawn
To that fair maid, whom he, in youth's full joy,
Had known and loved, whom now he found again,
The same and yet another, keeping still
The freshness of her girlhood, yet arrayed
In woman's graces. And he turned to her,
He whom Rome's fairest courted for their own,
Whom Galatea, sporting in the shade,
Hit with the golden fruit, while Flavia bent
The haughty pride of her patrician lips
In becks and smiles, and Domitilla fair,
In wild unwisdom, went with prayers and gold
To swarth Chaldæan sage and Marsian witch
For spells and love-charms. Yet they all were vain,
The smiles, the spells, the power of ancient name :

He chose the maid of Britain.   Whispers ran
Among his old companions, and they laughed
The evil laugh that speaks of evil heart ;   .
They pelted him with epigram and jest ;
But even they were somewhat held in check,
In awe of that great purity which beamed
From Claudia's presence.   Martial's licensed tongue
Found in her that which silenced scurril jest,
And woke faint pulses of the nobler heart,
The little life the canker had not killed :
And when the scourge of pleasant sins smote sore,
And he lay writhing in the grasp of pain
On fevered couch, he turned with piteous cry
To Pudens, as the one true friend of friends.
All jesting then was over; gibe and scoff,
Thrown back in answer to the kind reproof,
Were heard no more, but moans, and groans, and sighs,—
" Come to me, friend ; come, see me ere I die !"
And Pudens did not fail him, cooled the brow
That burnt with fever's torment, and stood by
Till all was over, and his soul passed on
In twilight to the judgment.
                         Soon the sky
Was dark with storms.   The tyrant's fury fell,
Sparing the people, on the chosen flock,
And Paul had fallen by the headsman's stroke,
And young Timotheos went to distant shores,
And came not back, and Phœbe and the rest

Were scattered far and wide, or swept away
In that fierce blaze of wrath.   But Pudens lived,
His name and rank protecting him, at peace,
Gave shelter as he could to wandering friends,
And, in the inner circle of his home,
Found rest and blessing.   Children came to him,
A daughter like her mother, and three sons,
Whom we baptized in secret, and I taught
Their infant lips to lisp their hymns to Christ,
And kept them from the evils of the time.
But oh ! my friends, that I could tell you half
Of Claudia's angel goodness !   Meek and pure,
She kept her path amid an evil world,
Diffusing light around her ; gems and gold
She would not wear, save that one circlet pure
That marked her as a matron, and the pearls,
Her country's growth, with which she bound her hair ;
But bore on clear, bright brow the costlier crown
Of tranquil meekness.   Clear and strong of will,
She ruled her household in the might of love ;
And we, her slaves, watched every nod and glance,
And did her bidding gently, no reward
Desiring but the beaming of her smile,
And, more than all the scourge's chastisement,
Fearing her sad, pale look of patient grief,
Turned as in pity.   Through the weary years
She nursed Pomponia's sad and lonely age,
With chanted psalms of ancient days, and prayers

That spoke out clearly what within her heart
Had brooded in confusion. But, ere long,
Her own turn came. Her northern life went out
Beneath the scorching of our summer south ;
And, ere her thirtieth summer came and went,
She faded from our sight. In vain we tried
The purer air where Anio pours his stream
O'er Tibur's rocks, or brought her to the coast
Where white sails glitter on the tideless sea.
She yearned for cooler clime, and fresher breeze ;
And, after some few months of fevered life,
Grew weak, and weaker yet. And Pudens nursed
That weakness to the last ; for he had learnt,
Beyond all spells of Aphrodite's charm,
Or wingèd Eros of the poet's dreams,
The meaning and the mystery of love,
And, in his Lord's great life of sacrifice,
That He might win a pure and spotless bride,
Saw the true law and archetype of his.
And then there came the end. The gathering mists
Of death were on her eyelids, and her thoughts
Ran back to spring-tide mornings of her youth :
She heard in dreams the ouzel and the lark,
The thrush and mavis of her native fields,
And sang wild songs of early Druid days ;
And then her true self saw and spoke again,
And, clinging fast to Pudens, who had held
Her hand in his through all the strife with death,

She whispered softly, " Closer, closer yet ;
Closer to thee and Him ! " and then one sigh,
And one sweet smile upon the thin, pale lips,
And all was over.   We, with prayer and hymn,
Bore her by night, with torches in our hands,
And laid her in the chambers of the dead,
Hard by the Appian.

                So her course was run,
Blessing and being blest, serene and clear
As star's bright orbit in the midnight gloom,
A strain of music in a world of storms.
And lo ! her death was mightier than her life :
That strain is echoing still with power to calm,
That star still sheds its glory from above ;
For Pudens, when the first lone weeks were past
Which crushed him with their weight of emptiness,
Rose from his sorrow stronger than before,
Seeking for nobler life, and loftier tasks,
To do his Master's bidding.   Dreary now
The glitter and the pageants of the world,
The legion's duties and the forum's strife.
He took the path that Linus trod before,
(Linus, true friend and brother of his youth,)
And gave himself to do his Master's work ;
And beautiful as are their feet who stand
Upon the mountains, and glad news proclaim
To all the listening thousands, so was seen
His presence, so were heard his words of peace.

And me he stirred to join him in that work,
And I, the slave, and he, the master, stood
Before our Elders, and they laid their hands
Upon our heads, and sent us forth to teach,
To watch and guide, encourage or restrain,
As need might call us.   Faithfully and well
Did Pudens keep his trust, stirred up our hearts
With hymns in which the speech of Greece became
A trumpet for the battle, spake good words
To souls that mourned, to young and old alike
Came as a brother.   Earnest, lofty look
Marked him as one who lived above the earth ;
And, though he sought no strife with those in power,
Nor, rushing to the market-place, reviled
The worship of his fathers, yet his voice
Was clear and firm to answer gibe or quest :
" I own myself a Christian."   Many a month
They spared him, out of homage to his name,
When others might have fallen ; but, at last,
A panic seized the people.   Rumours ran
Of secret meetings, schemes of frantic change,
And dark mysterious worship, (echoes weak
Of lies long since exploded ;) and our lord,
The Emperor, in his might, sent forth decrees
Of banishment or death against the sects
That spread new doctrine.   Pudens might have fled,
In safety hiding on Sardinian shores,
Or where Vesevus breathes its fiery smoke,

Until the storm was over; but he chose
To stay, and watch, and work, and meet the end
As God should send it.   And they tracked him out,
And led him to the Prætor, and from him
There came the sentence.   Tortures dread and foul,
Like those we knew in Nero's earlier time,
These they passed over, but the headsman's sword
Must do its work ; and so our Pudens fell,
Not as a martyr, 'mid the gazing crowd,
With yells and shouts that stir the blood to face
The foes of God with God's own panoply,
But secretly, in silence, so he fell ;
And then, by yon Gemonian steps, they cast
His body to the waters, and the stream
Bore it down yellow Tiber to the sea,
And then at Ostia, as the sunset fell,
It floated to the shore, and found a grave,
Which I alone, and some few others, know ;
Where, day by day, our friends break bread at night,
Pray for his peace, and, holding fast his faith,
Remember him with tears.
                              And now, farewell !
Ye have not yet resisted unto blood,
And better days are coming.   Soon enough
The fiery scourge will all be overpast,
This show of vigour soon be lulled to rest,
And ye once more may leave your hiding-place,
And seek your homes.   Far greater fear have I

Lest faith should falter, love be waxing cold,
And on your heart the world's contagion creep,
Like sorcerer's numbing potion. If ye feel
That spell upon you, break it at a bound ;
Lift up the feeble hands ; the weary feet
Send onward on their journey. Count it much
That you have known the lives of those that kept
Their soul's white pureness stainless from the world ;
And when men bid you to the feast and song,
And count it strange ye revel not with them,
Think ye upon their blameless lives who lived,
God's true light-bearers in a world of gloom,
And follow in the path that once was trod
By Claudia and by Pudens.

·*June* 1865.

THE RIVER.

DOWN-TRICKLING, soft and slow,
    Where the green mosses grow,
The baby streamlet hardly wakes the hush
    That broods o'er yonder height,
    Where falls the calm, low light,
And moor and peak give back the crimson flush.

    Then, as its waters swell,
    O'er crag, and rock, and fell,
They pour in many a thread of silver sheen ;
    And now their clearer voice
    Bids hill and vale rejoice,
And sweet, low echoes pierce the still serene.

    Wider and wider still,
    Half river and half rill,
The calmer current gladdens all the fields ;
    The banks are green and fair,
    And many a flow'ret bear,
And every breeze Æolian murmurs yields

There, in its golden bloom,
The cowslip breathes perfume,
Gray willows twist their branches hoar and brown ;
There sails in order meet
The ducklings' velvet fleet,
Or cygnet's argosy of golden down.

Past pleasant village-spire,
Past cheerful cottage fire,
In tranquil course flows on the nobler stream,
Spanned in its statelier march
By many a moss-grown arch,
Through which the sparkling ripples glance and gleam.

Now on its bosom float
White sails of fisher's boat,
Young swimmers stem the current swift and strong ;
Clear through the silent air
Ring voices free from care,
Youth's laughing shout and maiden's joyous song.

Onward past ancient halls,
Onward past castle-walls,
Each with wild legends of an earlier time,—
Stories of red-cross knight,
True to the death in fight,
Lay of true love, or darker tale of crime.

And now, on either side,
Rise, in exulting pride,
A city's turrets, palaces of state ;
The Minster's glorious tower
Looks down on hall and bower,
On fortress, market, churches, quay, and gate.

Broad sweeps the mightier flood,
Where once a forest stood,
Now all waste marish, fen, and reed-grown shore ;
And far on either hand
We see the distant sand,
And hear the sea's loud murmurs evermore.

Tall ships at anchor ride,
Their country's joy and pride,
And bring from East and West their priceless freight ;
All store of Nature's gifts
On that broad current drifts,
The decks are laden with the glorious weight.

Then flowing far and free
Into the boundless sea,
The yellow waters stain the crystal blue ;
At last its course is done,
And lo ! the westering sun
Floods sea and river with one roseate hue.

Flow on, ye rivers wide,
Welcome the changing tide,
Bear on your breast the costly argosy;
Flow, fountains, from the hill;
Flow, through thy meadow, rill;
Flow, baby streamlet, flow to yonder sea.

So flows our human life,
With mightier issues rife,
Onward and onward to a wider sea;
We note its feeble source,
We track its wandering course,
We know not what its destiny shall be.

Ah! well if it shall go,
With clear and crystal flow,
Rejoicing, gladdening, blessing still and blest;
In childhood, youth, and age,
Through all its pilgrimage,
Still hastening to the Ocean of its Rest.

But ah! if it shall waste,
Its strength in reckless haste,
The wild stream dashing to the depths below;
Or see, in dull decay,
All brightness fade away,
In marsh and fen half stagnate foul and slow.

Oh ! that our life might bear,
Sweet music to His ear,
Whom the great waters praise for evermore,
Attuned to anthems high,
In glorious harmony,
Till it too break upon the Eternal Shore.

April 1865.

"AND THERE WAS NO MORE SEA."*

"AND there was no more sea :"
    So spake the Prophet of the golden lips,
    Whose vision, clear and free,.
Saw the far depths of that Apocalypse.

    From each cavernous deep,
Where storms come not, and tempest wave is dumb,
    The forms of them that sleep
Shall rise undying when the Judge shall come.

    And then, its history o'er,
The great, wide sea shall flee and pass away,
    And many a golden shore,
Long hidden, greet the bright, eternal day.

    "No sea !" . . . . And shall the earth
Lose his loved bride, with all her countless smiles ?
    Shall that diviner birth
Destroy the beauty of her myriad isles ?

* Compare Bonar's *Hymns of Faith and Hope*, p. 10.

Shall that rich voice of praise,
Wide Ocean's anthem echoing to her Lord—
    That hymn of ancient days,
A thousand parts all met in sweet accord—

    Shall that be heard no more?
Shall all the beauty, all the glory flee?
    Shall the new earth's rich store
Lack the bright marvels of th' encircling sea?

    No! Far as man may dream
The wondrous glory yet to be revealed,
    Still on the eye shall gleam
The emerald waters as a crystal field;

    Still on the golden isles
The brightness of the Lord of light shall shine,
    And still the countless smiles
Illume the face of that clear hyaline.

    Only the drear expanse
Of waters barren, stormy, fathomless,
    Shall meet no more our glance,
Shall leave the new-born earth our souls to bless.

    No more the treacherous wave
Shall whelm poor wanderers in the homeless deep,

The dark and lonely grave
Where thousand shipwrecked souls have slept their sleep.

No more the billows wild
Shall hurl white breakers on the rock-bound coast ;
    By mightiest spell beguiled,
Slumbers each form of all the monster host.

Leviathan is tamed
Who scorned the waters in his pride of strength ;
    And now no more is named
Where once he measured all his monstrous length.

But still the ear shall greet
The music of the ever-rippling wave,
    And where the waters meet,
The crystal tide the palm-girt shore shall lave.

Crowned high with amaranth grove,
The hills shall rise by man and angels trod ;
    The ocean of His love
Shall still make glad the city of our God.

When Eden's bowers were green,
We knew not how the four great rivers wound
    Those glorious fields between,
Or circling took their wide majestic round

To lands renowned of old—
Cush, Asshur, Havilah, whence came the spice,
    The onyx, and the gold—
Yet watered still the groves of Paradise.

    We know not how the light
Shall flow when neither sun nor moon shall shine ;
    And yet no shade of night
Shall mar the glory of the blaze divine.

    We know not how the streams
Of those great rivers shall flow wide and free ;
    And yet the Prophet's dreams
Proclaim aloud, " There shall be no more sea."

    We know not . . . but the veil
Which hides it from our sight shall one day lift,
    And, where in vision pale
As yet the darkness and the storm-clouds drift,

    God shall make all things new,
And shoreless sea shall join with sealess shore ;
    And cleansèd eyes shall view
Might, wisdom, mercy, met for evermore.

April 1865.

AN OLD STORY.

I.—A.D. 1117.

I MISS thy voice, dear friend. The hours are long,
   And vexing thoughts bewilder. Wilt thou give
Thy counsel to thy pupil? None save thee
Can guide me through the tangled maze and dark ;
No eye but thine see clearly through the mist ;
No voice so breathe, in music of sweet sounds,
The wisdom that ennobles. As it is,
Again I travel o'er the path we trod,
Read the same books, at evening and at morn
Remember thee in every orison,
And count the hours till thou come back again,
And, bright as is the sunlight on the hills,
Thy presence shine on me. Meantime I ask
That insight which, through earth, and heaven, and
   deep,
Finds nothing hidden, soars above the stars
With wing that never flags, to spare for me
The crumbs that from the rich man's banquet fall
To glut the beggar's hunger. I would know

The mystery of our reason and our speech :
These words of ours, that speak of truth and good,
Man, angel, God ; . . . what are they ?   May we hold
God gave them to us, outward signs of things
That lie within the veil ?   Has every name,
So lightly used, its primal archetype
Eternal in the heavens ?   And do we reach
'Through them the living truth, our " good" and "fair"
The symbols of a beauty and a good
We yet scarce dream of?   Or, rejecting that,
As but itself a dream which mocks the thought
With visions of a world which is not ours,
Which altogether is not, must we treat
These words with which we travel high and far,
As but the coinage of our minting brain,
Fools' money, wise men's counters ?   And if so,
Why cheat our souls with all this endless toil,
This weary strife of tongues, when yet at last
We get no nearer to the living truth,
(If truth there be,) but play an infant's game,
Destroying, building, all our systems fair
Houses of cards that rise and have their day,
And never shelter give to weary souls,
Nor keep their ground against the storms of time ?
I pass o'er other questions.   May we hold
Our numbers, measures, weights as patterns drawn
From that high Wisdom which has ordered all,
This goodly world, yon firmament of stars,

By number, weight, and measure ?   Music's laws,
So wondrous in their working, giving voice
To thoughts that lie beyond the grasp of words,
To feelings deep below the fount of tears,
Are they too echoes of a nobler song,
The spheral music of the circling stars,
The anthems of the angels ?

                          Passing these,
I hasten on and upward.   Holier ground
I dare to tread on, look with eager eye
Where angels veil their faces, shrink not back
From boldest searching.   Once I lived my life,
As others live, in girlhood's reverent fear ;
Matins and vespers drew my thoughts to God ;
I prayed the saints to shield my soul from harm ;
Our Lady smiled from out her gilded shrine,
And won me with her beauty.   Feast and Fast
Brought their due changes as the seasons ran,
And I observed them in the childlike faith
That this was all my duty.   Then thy form
Rose, like a meteor on the darkened sky ;
Thou camest, Master mine, and lo ! thy words
Were as a key to ope the secret store
Of Wisdom's treasures.   Now the wondrous thoughts
Of Prophet and Apostle clearer grew ;
The words and deeds of Him above them both
Were as an open scroll ; and so we tracked
The march of Truth across the waste of Time,

Fair, glorious, terrible, as though we saw
An army with its banners. Many a name
That led the vanguard of that mighty host
Became to us familiar. Jerome first,
Who wrought his task in Bethlehem's holy cave,
And from his cell did govern women's hearts,
Marcella, Paula, as thy lightest word
Has governed mine. And then Augustine came,
Wild, reckless, wandering, till the mighty prayer
Of Monica prevailed, and all the flood
Of wild desire lay calm, and clear, and hushed,
And mirrored back the likeness of his Lord,
As sleeping waters in a mountain lake
Give back the golden sunlight. Origen,
Him too we read of, with his wondrous hope,
Wide-spreading o'er the universe of God,
And purgèd eyes that saw behind the veil
Of outward symbol. Nor was other food
Wanting in those our banquets. Virgil told
His tale of great Æneas, and the love,
Impassioned, fatal, of the Tyrian queen,
Or how the minstrel seer of old sought out,
And found, and lost, his loved Eurydice.

Ah, friend! thou too hast found, ... and wilt thou
      lose ?
Thy music's spell has roused my soul from sleep
That was as death, and shall thy eager glance,

Thy love's wild frenzy, passionate embrace,
Hurl me to death again ?   No ; go thy way ;
Be to the world what thou hast been to me,
Dispel the darkness, bid the discords hush,
Give truth free speech, and rise to all the height
Of thy great calling.   Men admire thee now ;
They list with rapture to thy honeyed speech ;
Old dotards curse thee, and the bold and young
Own thee their master.   Go and conquer then ;
March onward till thou reach the dizzy peak
Of lonely power, and from the apostle's throne
Put forth thine arm with power to bind or loose ;
Smite thou the kings and mighty ones of earth,
Shield thou the poor who delve and toil for bread,
Break thou the bonds and set the captives free :
Be as the Prophet-Priest of this our day,
And with thy bright cloud-piercing intellect,
Lead thou the Church, through all the dreary waste,
The land of wanderings, to the brighter hopes,
The vision of the future.   And for me,
When this shall be, and I, in lowliest shade,
Have found my refuge, I will sometimes ask
In evening's dreams, "And does he think of me,
 Whom once he guided up the slopes of Truth,
And do his prayers rise up, as mine for him,
For her who loved him . . . ."   Yes, the word must pass,
" With love so eager, passionate, intense,
That it would fain forget itself in death,

And be as though it were not?"   To renounce
All honour, hope, enjoyment, welcome shame,
Reproach, and solitude ; no more to see
The face so loved, nor hear the voice that thrills
The inmost soul ; for very love's dear sake
To crush love out, that so no cloud may come
Between thee and thy fortunes ;—this be mine,
And thine be . . . . what God sends thee.

II.—A.D. 1142.

And so that life is ended.   Rest at last,
After long wandering on the troubled sea,
Comes to the sailor shipwrecked, tempest-tost ;
The fevered sufferer sinks to dreamless sleep,
And never more shall that clear eye flash fire,
Against his foes or mine, nor that strong voice
Rise high above the babbling strife of tongues,
In mightiest self-assertion.   Bernard now
May leave his dust to moulder in the grave,
And rest in peace.   And I, who hear, am calm ;
No master-passion melts my soul in tears,
My sorrow does not overflow its bounds.
My heart is calm to search and scan its grief.
Yes !   I who once found all my world in him,
Who for him lost fair fame, and holy peace,
Who night and morning dreamt of nought but him,
Who breathed his name in every secret prayer,

I hear the tidings, " He at last is gone,"
As though 'twere but a neighbour whom one greets,
From week to week with nod of kindly mood,
And else knows nought of.

                Yet with him there lies
All that my soul once knew of light and warmth,
All the bright day-dreams of my opening life ;
Long since they died, and in the grave of love
Embalmed I laid them.   Now the vault is oped
That he may lie there.   Soon the years shall bring
Their longed-for end, and then the shadowy gates,
Thrown wide, shall welcome me.   Meantime I live,
And do my work, and travel o'er the past,
And weigh and scan his merits who was once
The idol of my passion.   Now I see
How poor the idol, how the head of gold
Passed on to baser metal, mire and clay ;
The lordly, wide-embracing intellect
To low desire, that tainted, poisoned all,
The canker that devoured the goodliest bloom
And made it fruitless.   So, alas ! it was
With him, with me.   The noblest gifts of God,
The worthiest work as vessel of the Truth,
He cast aside, flung reckless in the mire,
Lost his true life, and left Christ's chosen bride
For me, poor frail one.   Dare I murmur now
That this all vanished like a fevered dream,
And had its stern awakening, that for me

Came scorn, reproach, life worn before its time,
Hair gray, cheeks faded, sky o'ercast and dim,
The throbbings of a heart that will not heal.
Yes, I have paid the forfeit.   Not for me
The blessing which the poorest peasant wife
Finds in the name of Mother: guilt and shame,
These threw their shadows o'er my new-born joy,
And he, my child, my boy, my Astrolabe,
(Name telling of ill stars and evil days,)
Was taken from me.   Not for me the bliss
Of infant's lips, soft touch, and joyous smile:
I might not part the golden locks that streamed
On either side the clear and noble brow,
Nor teach the soul its song of joy and praise,
Nor when the boy was ripening to the man,
Receive the homage, hearty, frank, and true
Of son to mother.   Far and far away,
Beyond the frozen snows on Alpine heights,
The boy grew up ; and now the man lives on,
And little knows the story of his birth,
Nor heeds the prayers which, day by day, rise up
Like incense from the altar of my heart.

This was my heavy burden : and for him,
The partner of my passion and my sin,
A ceaseless strife of fightings and of fears,
Wrong past all speech, a life without a home,
Fame grasping its own shadow, bitter hate

K

From those who loved the darkness more than light ;
Or, harder still to bear, distrust and grief
From those who loved the light, and lived in truth,
And saw in him the root of every ill,
A will self-centred, scorn of lowlier souls,
The pride that in the chambers of its heart
Sets up its secret idols ?   No, my God,
I give Thee thanks for all.   There might have been
Far heavier judgment.   Thicker veil of night
Might still have hid the evil.   Fame and power
Might have been his beyond his heart's desire,
Chief place among the shepherds of the flock,
Gray hairs, full honour, and a name to live
Among the saints of God.   Ah ! tenfold worse
That life of semblance with its show of health,
Its inward rottenness, than all the pain,
The sharp, keen goads that gave not rest nor peace
Until their work was done, and all the soul
Was cleansed and humbled. False those dreams of yore ;
Truth's chosen ones are cast in other mould,
Her victories won by other strategy ;
No skill of speech, nor daring, prompt to try
New paths through all the cloud-girt Infinite,
No life where sense and soul hold equal sway,
And soon sense masters soul.   Her seal is set
On those who love her for herself alone,
Who woo with lowly heart her favouring smile,
And seek her wisdom secretly ; pure souls,
On whom no touch of sense has left its stain,

Who go their way through gathering mists and clouds,
Light-bearers in the darkness.   They can own
God's footprints in the story of the past,
His love through all the present, and, far off,
Hail the bright future.   Once I dreamt that he
Would bear that light, and, foremost, near the throne,
Take rank with those, the star-crowned cherubim,
Excelling most in knowledge.   Now I see,
His name upon the charts of life shall stand
To tell of shoals on which the noblest ship
Made utter wreck, and men shall point to it,
Some, half in scorn, and some, in tenderer grief,
" Lo ! this was Abelard."
                Be mine the shame,
If spirits hear from out the gates of death
The converse of the living, still to bear
That long, long penance of a tainted name,
The sin remembered, all the rest forgot ;
Only do Thou, divinest Paraclete,
Who dost not scorn the bruised and contrite heart,
To whom we turned in bitterness of soul,
Only do Thou give wisdom, e'er the night
Shall fall, to do Thy work, Thy freedom give,
And though the cares that harass and perplex,
Give patience, meekness, hope ; and thus, at last,.
Cleanse this poor heart from all its earthly love,
And fill it with the love that changes not,
The Charity Eternal.

April 1865.

EUMENIDES.

WEIRD shapes of fear and dread,
  With shadowy wings outspread,
On felon footsteps following sure and swift;
  Fierce eyes that wildly glance,
  Like lightning flames, askance,
Through the thick darkness where the storm-clouds
    drift.

  Harsh voice of fearful power,
  In midnight's silent hour
Waking sad echoes of departed times;
  Recalling hate and greed,
  The thought, the word, the deed,
Youth's maddening joy and manhood's darker crimes.

  O'er rivers flowing fast,
  O'er mountains hoar and vast,
Chasing their victim with a blood-hound's bay,
  Their keen, unearthly yell,
  Of hope and joy the knell,
Startles the trembler crouching far away.

For ever on his track,
For ever at his back,
Their long gaunt fingers clutch his mantle's hem ;
Vain is the sevenfold shield,
Vain are the swords men wield,
Vain purple robe, and kingly diadem.

In festive hall, or bower,
In mirth's exulting hour,
The spectral sisters meet his shuddering eye :
When solemn music clear,
Falls softly on his ear ;
Alone, or when the gathering throng sweeps by.

Can man no secret find,
Their dark, dread power to bind,
And lull their fury to perpetual sleep ?
Or must he ever bear
The weight of chill despair,
While still their watch the stern Erinnyes keep ?

Yes, seers and sages old,
The mystic rites have told,
That fixed, avenging purpose to appease ;
Man, meekly bending low,
Accepting all his woe,
May find the anguish soften into peace.

First, let him take his stand,
Green boughs in either hand,
Where from the rock the living water flows ;
The pure libation pour,
The awful Powers adore,
Then turn to where the dark rich laurel grows.

There slowly through the shade
Of each o'erarching glade,
With trembling footsteps let him seek the shrine ;
Then, bending low, confess
Their power to curse or bless,
Himself all vile, their justice all divine.

No purpling wine-cup there
Must taint the clear, calm air,
Though glowing clusters darken all the earth ;
No pæan loud and long
Must wake exulting song,
No revel wild and free wake shouts of mirth.

But cries of grief and prayer,
One note above despair,
And eyes still fixed upon the judgment throne ;
The slow retreating tread,
The memories of the dead,
The heart that fain would all the past atone.

So, as the suppliant kneels,
A wondrous calmness steals
O'er those dread faces gleaming through the grove ;
Gone is the angry frown,
The avenging hands hang down,
The Wrath divine is melting into Love.

The voice for vengeance loud,
The thunder from the cloud,
Melt into murmurs of a distant sea,
When zephyrs soft and low,
Beneath the sunset's glow,
Wake in each wave its voice of minstrelsy.

The eyes that flashed with fire,
Rebuking foul desire,
Are grave and pitying with a milder light ;
They watch and they approve
The sorrow and the love
Which guide the wanderer's footsteps through the
night.

So, evermore the same,
They change their mood and name,
No more the dread Erinnyes, sound of fear ;
Eumenides, the kind,
The gentle ones in mind,
They smooth the brow, and wipe away the tear.

Thus, in her visions dim,
Old Hellas dreamt of Him,
The Avenger and Forgiver, whom we know,
Watching the shifting skies,
With varying auguries,
Now lit with hope, now clouded o'er with woe.

So must each thought of ill,
Bear its due scourging still,
The keen, sharp iron must pierce unto the soul ;
The avenging fire must burn,
The torturing hour return,
The waves and billows o'er the spirit roll.

But when the heart shall bend
Its stubborn will, the end
Shall gleam in joy and brightness as the morn ;
Bowed low before its God,
To kiss the chastening rod,
Hope dawns once more on features pale and worn.

Here, too, the cleansing flood
Of water and of blood,
Must wash the suppliant from the deep-dyed stain ;
He, on the hallowed ground,
Must walk in awe profound,
And through the darkness pass to light again.

Here too no revel mirth
Must bring the songs of earth,
To mar the silence which the angels love ;
Only the bitter cry,
" Lord, save us, or we die,"
This shall at once our prayer and anthem prove.

So shall the two-edged sword,
The Spirit's mighty word,
Smite but to heal the poor, sin-stricken heart ;
So from the Judge's face,
Shall smile of pardoning grace
Bring joy and gladness to the wounds that smart.

So shall the Eternal Name,
Though changing, still the same,
Be to the soul its everlasting shield ;
The King hath turned away
His Judgment's fiery day,
To children poor and weak the Father stands revealed.

February 1865.

A PLASTER CAST FROM POMPEII.

[In recent excavations at Pompeii, the dust in which the city was entombed was found to have taken the mould of the bodies of a group of men,
women, and children, who appeared to have taken refuge in the court-yard
of a villa. To remove the mould was impossible, but plaster of Paris was
poured in, and the casts thus obtained (one of them, that of a girl of sixteen
or seventeen) are now in the Museum there.—*Revue des deux Mondes*,
xlvii. p. 231.]

ONCE I was young and fresh,
    Fair with the fairest ;
Now thou who standest there
    Know'st not, nor carest :
Then the youths sang my praise,
    Flushed with the dancing ;
Now thine eye coldly falls,
    Here and there glancing.

Lo ! the hot air was thick,
    Stifling and steaming ;
Through the gray mist the sun
    Rose, dimly gleaming.
Then a wild flash of fire,
    Crash as of thunder ;
All faces black with fear,
    All sick with wonder.

Then the white dust fell fast,
   Blinding our vision ;
Men who had feared the Gods
   Mocked in derision ;
Mockers in fear fell down,
   Death's spell upon them ;
Gamesters threw up their dice ;
   Hades had won them.

Hushed was the minstrel's song,
   Stiff grew the lithest ;
All the stout hearts waxed faint,
   Awe-struck the blithest ;
I to my mother ran,
   Love's shelter seeking ;
Men sought their wives and babes,
   Gasping, not speaking.

Still the hot dust came down,
   Choking our breath then,
And on our hearts there fell
   Darkness of death then :
Friends, mothers, children fled,
   In the dark meeting,
Whispering, ere life had fled,
   Last words of greeting.

Flowers in my hair were twined,
  Gracefully braided,
Now by the scorching blast,
  Withered and faded ;
Necklet of gold I wore,
  Pearls that I cherished,—
These thou hast looked on here,
  All else has perished.

I to the court-yard gate
  Rushed in my madness,
After wild throbs of dread,
  Fear conquering sadness ;
There were they met, my friends,
  Father and mother,
Faithful slave, lover true,
  Sister and brother.

So we faced death at last,
  Each to each clinging ;
Some, in their wild despair,
  Frenziedly singing ;
Most with clenched hands and lips,
  Stiffened with sorrow :
We, who were met there then,
  Saw no to-morrow.

Bright was the life we lived:
   This was its ending.
Had we provoked the Gods,
   Blindly offending?
Did they look down in wrath,
   Jealously grudging?
Did they chastise our guilt,
   Righteously judging?

Long had those fires of hell
   Peacefully slumbered;
Men lived, and toiled, and loved,
   Years none had numbered:
Now the dread doom came on,
   Sent without warning;
Sunk in the night of death,
   Where was our morning?

Gladly our years had passed,
   Buying and selling,
Dancing with pipe and harp,
   Lovers' tales telling:
Now the fierce wrath of Gods
   Dried up life's fountain;
Fire-streams none knew till then
   Flowed from yon mountain.

One there was, even then,
  Tranquil, unaltered ;
Calmly he looked on death,
  Voice had not faltered ;
Strange in his blood and speech,
  Men looked with jeering ;
Girls, in their pride of heart,
  Shrank back, half fearing.

Now as we sank in death
  Came his voice clearer,
First sounding far away,
  Then near, and nearer ;
Voice, as of one who prays,
  Eagerly pleading,
For friends, and foes, and all,
  Still interceding.

" So once of old the fire
  Burst on Lot's city ;
So Thou dost smite us now,
  Lord of all pity.
Through all the crowds I see,
  Aged or youthful,
Not ten, nor five are found,
  Righteous and truthful.

" Yet, Lord, have mercy now,
   Spare those who perish ;
Take them, and teach them, Lord,
   Chasten and cherish :
Babes in the dawn of life,
   Youths in its morning,
Thou hast redeemed them, Lord,
   Not one soul scorning."

Such were the words we heard,
   Strengthening and cheering ;
So we sank down to sleep,
   Hoping, yet fearing :
Just for one breath we knew
   What death's strange calm meant,
Then we were safe entombed,
   Dust our embalmment.

Now we lie side by side,
   None knows our story,
What has come after death,
   Darkness or glory;
None reads the lesson right,
   Awe-struck with wonder,
Though these clay lips might speak
   Louder than thunder.

Go thou, who standest there,
  Tranquilly dreaming,
Learn the stern truths that lie
  Under all seeming.
Feeding the pride of life,
  Thou thyself starvest ;
Thine is the seed-time now ;
  Whose is the harvest ?

July 1865.

THE LAST WORDS OF SOCRATES.

" We owe a cock to Æsculapius."

NO scorn or doubt was thine, O martyred one,
   Nor feigned compliance with accustomed rite.
But faith, in that last hour, serenely bright,
Through smile half-sad, and jest half-earnest, shone.
Rich rays of glory crown the westering sun ;
   And thou, thy long day's journey all but o'er,
   Casting one glance from that eternal shore,
Thy crown of light, thy better life had'st won. ·
No draught Nepenthè, quick and strong to soothe,
   Vied with that hemlock in its power to save,
And dim eyes, opening on th' unveilèd Truth,
   Saw the far land that lies beyond the grave ;
Hushed into silence man's perpetual strife,
All healed by death the long disease of life.

June 1865.

L

A VOICE FROM OXFORD.

———◆———

ON, noblest statesman thou of all our time,
    On to the tasks that lie before thee still,
  To guide, control, raise, purify the will
Of toiling millions in their manhood's prime.
Thy flight soars high above the cloudy clime
    Where dull tradition holds her wonted sway,
    And those who haunt the twilight hate the day,
And fear and sloth still lag behind the time.
We miss thee now, but England owns her son,
    Tried in the fire that purifies the gold :
Ours is the loss, but thou hast nobly won ;
    Then on, be brave, the future's scroll unfold,
And, as the months of ordered progress run,
    From out thy treasures bring forth new and old

July 1865.

MOZART'S ZAUBERFLÖTE.

OH, onward tread of those who march victorious,
    Oh', sound of triumph surging like a sea ;
Thrills through the soul thy *Jubilate* glorious,
    And fears and doubts, and dreams and shadows flee.

So Israel's armies marched through gleaming waters,
    When Amram's son bade all their hosts advance ;
So Miriam led her troop of Israel's daughters,
    Chanting loud praise with timbrel and with dance.

So march the warriors who, for freedom fighting,
    Have borne the brunt of battle, fierce and hot ;
Brave hearts, stout arms, in serried ranks uniting,
    Though thousand foes are round them, fearing not.

So upward wend their way, on Truth's high mountain,
   Her chosen knights, through storm and wind and cold,
Their soiled feet bathing in her clear, calm fountain,
   That flows like crystal over sands of gold.

So those that press through shadows thick and darkling,
   O'er heath and moor, o'er wild and waste who roam,
As morning breaks, behold the bright sea sparkling,
   Clear path that bears them to their distant home.

Ah me ! too soon the echoes fast are fleeting,
   Too soon the dull, cold heart forgets its glow,
In craven fear from each high task retreating,
   In faithless weakness shrinking from the foe.

The shadows gather round us thickly falling,
   Hover and shriek foul birds of evil wing,
Now here, now there, our wandering footsteps calling,
   And spectral forms dark thoughts of terror bring.

How shall we sing the song of joy abounding,
   On whom there rests the curse of vanished years ?
How shall we triumph, in whose ears are sounding,
   Whispers that startle, cries that fill with fears ?

Yet, onward press, faint heart, too weakly yielding,
   Still let the music speak of hope and strength ;

Thy path the outspread wings of God are shielding,
  And thou shalt reach thy Father's home at length.

Steep though the path be, rough the winds that chill thee,
  Starless the night, the tempest wild and loud,
Still let the echoes of that high strain thrill thee,
  And guide thee safely through the mist and cloud.

Oh, onward tread of those who march victorious,
  Oh, sound of triumph surging like a sea,
So let us hear thy *Jubilate* glorious,
  So let all fears, dreams, doubts, and shadows flee.

September 1855.

NOT WITHOUT WITNESS.

I.

SCENOPEGIA.

I.

COME, gather boughs of palm,
Down in the groves where Jordan winds his way;
    Or, breathing airs of balm,
Pluck the dark myrtle's snowy-blossomed spray;

    Pines from the lofty height,
Where roam the wolf and bear on Hermon's hill,
    Or willow gleaming white,
Where sleep the moonbeams on the waters still;

    Yes, bring them one and all,
And on the roof, beneath the autumn sky,
    What time the trumpets call,
Wreathe, twist, and twine the leafy canopy.

    There, as the sun sinks low,
And purpling glory flashes all the West,

In solemn cadence slow
Chant the old hymn that speaks of peace and rest :

There, when the clouds unfold,
Far in the East, the tints of opening dawn,
And Ophir's fiery gold
Is poured from Heaven on each high mountain lawn,

There raise the anthem clear,
The Hallelujahs by our fathers sung,
And, spreading far and near,
Let the loud chorus pour from every tongue.

2.

Up, rise ye, rise, with shouts of joy,
From man and woman, maid and boy ;
For lo ! the circling autumn sun
His long year's course has all but run.
Right well the teeming womb of earth
Has given to man its wondrous birth ;
All now is ours, and nothing lacks,
The first ripe barley, latest flax ;
On every wide-spread threshing-floor
The wheat sheaves yield their golden store,
And patient oxen, as they tread,
Leave the clear grain for staff of bread.
From out the olives, as we press,
There flows, our wearied limbs to bless,

The crystal stream of golden oil,
Rich guerdon of the labourer's toil ;
And, last and best, from Eshcol's vine
We drain the sweet, soul-quickening wine.
Through all the joyous crowds that throng
Our vineyards float the sounds of song,
And goodliest youths the winepress tread,
Their feet and garments stained with red.
What time the heathen, flushed and wild,
By dreams and fancies foul beguiled,
In frenzied dance or whirling maze,
With pinewood torches' flashing blaze,
Dance to the god, the child of Jove,
And sing of mirth, and joy, and love ;
What time the Mænads' sharp, shrill cry
Breaks the calm silence of the sky,
And locks dishevelled, wine-besprent,
Fall down o'er faces passion-spent,
And wearied frames convulsed, possessed,
At last sink, panting, into rest,
Behold our priests in robes of white,
Inwrought with blue and scarlet bright,
From Siloa's well to Zion turn,
Uplifting high their golden urn ;
And there before the altar-stairs,
With chants of praise and loud-voiced prayers,
Pour forth, in sight of Israel,
The waters from salvation's well ;

And when at eve the darkness falls
O'er street and market, huts and halls,
Behold one lamp, with mightiest blaze,
Shed far and wide its fiery rays,
O'er temple, court, and crowded street,
Where pilgrims haste with busiest feet,
Down Kedron's valley, further yet
O'er yon steep slope of Olivet.

What soul so hard, and dead, and cold,
So deaf to all our fathers told,
As not to give to sick and poor
Free offering from its plenteous store?
Let friends greet friends with open hand,
Let each the other's purse command,
Let gifts be tokens true and clear
Of loving hearts, and friendship dear,
And anger die, as dies the year.
Each thought unkind, each harboured grudge
In his own heart let each man judge;
Cast out the unripe grapes and wild,
The clusters tainted and defiled:
There in the vineyard given to thee
Let root, branch, tendril cleansèd be;
Tread thou the wine-press till there flow
The fragrant stream with orient glow,
Which, pouring still as first it ran,
Makes glad the heart of God and man.

3.

So kept the feast our fathers long ago,
    When first in Canaan's soil
Their hands a harvest reaped they did not sow,
    Won without sweat of toil.

So through long years the kings of David's line,
    Who with their fathers sleep,
Revering still the oracle divine,
    That feast were wont to keep.

Ah! did they dream of secret, mystic truth
    Beneath the outer veil;
Or did our sires in manhood as in youth
    Live on the thrice-told tale?

Was it with backward look upon the past,
    When they from Egypt came,
When tents were spread through all the desert vast
    Around the central flame?

Or did they dream of all life's little span
    As of a traveller's tent,
Of all the joys that crown the life of man
    As garlands dew-besprent;

The journey through the wilderness of years
    As theirs who seek a rest,

And take their pilgrim path through vale of tears,
    As yet but partly blest?

Or looked they forward to a time to come,
    In dim, far future seen,
When all, as yet enwrapt in symbols dumb,
    Shall shine in light serene;

And as, of old, the countless homes were spread
    O'er deserts far and wide,
While yet one tent on all its glory shed,
    For God did there abide;

So shall one form on all the sons of men
    Pour brightness from the throne,
The Word Eternal dwelling with us then
    Us as his brothers own;

One chosen tent wherein the presence dwells
    Of light and love divine,
While every soul the tale of wonder tells,
    Or sprung from Abraham's line,

Heir of his name, and child of Israel,
    Within the chosen race,
Or seed of heathens under sin's dark spell,
    Then sharing God's great grace?

II.

DIONYSIA.

I.

See, over Sunium's height the golden Morn
   Gleams, stretching forth her rosy-fingered hand,
   And o'er the smiling waves, and vine-clad land,
Sheds the rich lustre of the light new born.

At break of day they haste from every deme,
   Kolonos, Parnes, or Acharnæ old;
   Where shepherds seek the wanderers from their fold,
By fair Ilissos, or Kephisos' stream;

Where slopes Hymettos with its fragrant store,
   Or sacred pathway to Eleusis leads,
   Where plane-trees whisper to the answering reeds,
Or rich Laureion yields her silvern ore;

They haste in festive garments through the street,
   By Agora, and Pnyx, and Parthenon,
   And ere the dew has yielded to the sun,
In the great court of Dionysos meet.

For now fair Spring has come with smiles and mirth,
   And green the grass on meadow and on hill,
   With sweeter music flows each mountain rill,
And showers and zephyrs gladden all the earth.

Here where, of old, our fathers met and sang
  In rude, wild hymns the mirth and might divine
  Of Bacchus, child of Zeus, and lord of wine,
And jest and song through all the clear air rang ;—

Here now we own the Lord of life and song,
  Giving high thoughts, and kindling poet's fire,
  With roseate flush just warming young desire,
The Lord and Master of the Muses' throng.

From every legend of the storied past,
  Man's wrath and sorrow, penitence and guilt,
  Crime wrought in darkness, blood at random spilt,
The dread Erinnys' vengeance following fast ;—

Stories of Thebes, of Argos, and of Troy,
  These come before us framed by poet's skill,
  From choral lips the songs of homage thrill,
Waking or fear or pity, grief or joy.

So wise men's hearts have widened with the years,
  And rude, rough revel yields to loftier thought ;
  We own and praise the gladness all unsought ;
But joy is noblest when it blends with tears.

The Giver of the gladness of the vine,
  We own Him Lord of all that stirs and warms,

The song that soothes, the strain that calls to
    arms,
The choral dance, the hymn before the shrine.

2.

Yes, come, ye Mænads, floating hair
Cast wildly to the midnight air;
With flashing eye, and blazing torch,
Rush wildly on through columned porch;
"Evöe," shout; "Evöe" still,
In dusky grove, by warbling rill;
Wake up the echoes far and near,
Bid all the fawns and satyrs hear,
Sing ye the song men sang of old
When from the yeanlings of the fold,
They brought the goat to Bacchus' shrine,
Foe of the tendrils of the vine.
Dance ye, dance wildly in your joy,
Mirth that our God gives cannot cloy.
This glow that warms the old man's veins,
With gleams of sunlight after rains,
This flush that mantles youth's fair face
With kindling eye and roseate grace,
And bids the boy cast off his fears,
And know a life beyond his years,
What is all this, with wonder rife,
But nature's magic, life of life,
That works through sun, and moon, and star,
With subtle stirrings near and far,

Sends the fresh sap through budding grove,
Bids every leaf and floweret move,
And perfect grows in youth's first love?
With mightiest touch that wondrous spell
Makes blossoms open, fruitage swell,
Draws forth from nightingale and lark
The songs that charm the light and dark;
On Psyche's fluttering wings outpours
The orient tints of star-paved floors,
And through the veins of nobler forms
Rushes, as rush the sweeping storms,
To find, at last, its noblest prey
When men bow down before its sway,
And fill the throbbing heart and brain
With joy so keen it ends in pain.

Right well our festal games to-day
Should all the mystic power display;
The frolic mirth, the frenzy wild,
Mirth of the savage and the child;
Where, strained in rapture, every sense
Seems bursting with the joy intense,
And brute-like stirrings through us thrill,
Unguided by the loftier will;
Let satyrs sport with laughing fawns,
In sheltered groves, on mountain lawns,
Crowned with the ivy and the vine,
Goat-limbed, and faces red with wine.

So let it be, but holier sound
Must in the solemn rite be found ;
To Him, the son of Zeus, far-famed,
The God of Nysa, many-named,
Must rise the choral song of praise,
Our heritage from ancient days ;
Nor can we spare the mystic art,
Which stirs the throbbings of the heart,
Tells the dark tale of woe sublime,
The havoc of the conqueror, Time ;
Or tracks, in sequence dark and strange,
Life's varied course of chance and change.

So, when the crimson sun has set,
And all the vines with dews are wet ;
When stars obey their leader's call,
And round the moon keep festival,
The long, long day within its span
Shall hold complete the life of man,
Its instincts, passions, thrilling sense,
Its calm and clear intelligence ;
The bands that bind him still to earth,
The hopes that speak a loftier birth.
Alone, of all beneath the sky,
He lives, half brute, half deity ;
In him the darkness blends with day,
The gold, thrice cleansed, with mire and clay ;
And so from morning unto eve,
The varied web of life we weave ;

Hues of the rainbow, gleams of fire,
Joy, sorrow, hope, despair, desire;
And, as the shuttle to and fro
We ply, the strains of music flow,
· And speak, now soft as fountain's fall,
Now mighty as the storm-cloud's call,
The life that stirs in infant's breath,
And, all paths traversed, ends in death.

2.

It was not all a dream,
That vision of a power to stir and move,
Which sheds its joyous gleam,
And fills the world and man with life,and love.

The purple juice that flows
From cask or skin in goblet wrought with gold,
Whose rich, dark ruby glows,
Like purple sunset on a temple old,

Is parable and type
Of holiest things that lie within the veil;
Those clusters full and ripe
Tell of a Spirit mighty to prevail.

He once, whom we adore,
Took bread and brake, and to the Twelve He gave,

M

The Paschal supper o'er,
The wine that told of life from out the grave.

Of all God's gifts to man
That only filled the measure of the truth,
Witness of life that ran
Through years and changes with unfailing youth ;

Witness of holier life,
Whose joy bursts out in hymn, and chant, and psalm,
And, through the world's rough strife,
Bids storm-tossed souls take courage and be calm.

He, who the winepress trod,
Who poured His blood as wine of sacrifice,
And in His zeal for God,
And love for man, paid their full ransom-price ;

He gives His life-blood still,
Joy of all joys, and solace of all woe,
Man's heart and soul to fill,
In gushing stream through every vein to flow.

When on the chosen band
There came the sound of rushing, mighty wind,
And flames, on either hand,
Disparted, and strange speech of newest kind ;

Men laughed, and mocked, and said:
" Lo ! these are drunken, all unfit to teach,
New wine hath filled each head ;
See, here the secret of their babbling speech."

And half their words were right,
For then, in that high ecstasy divine,
That flashing of new light,
Their souls grew dizzy, drunk, but not with wine.

And so through every age,
The life that works through Nature and through man
Here gains its highest stage,
As upward from the old great deeps it ran.

Yes, He, the Lord of life,
Who brooded o'er the waste of waters wild,
And calmed their war and strife,
He comes with breath as whispering and as mild

As breeze of summer morn ;
And wakes new music, pours the floods of song
Through heart and soul new-born,
And all, by that great current swept along,

Know joy ne'er felt before,
A peace unbroken that is not of earth ;

While through the sere heart pour
Rivers of gladness, streams of heavenly mirth.

They own in prayer and vow,
How poor the bliss that thrilled the eager sense;
The good wine kept till now,
Bursting the vessel with the joy intense.

And so when all shall meet
At wedding-feast, in garments white and clean,
And at their Lord's dear feet
Shall see Him as He is, no veil between,

Then they shall drink new wine,
As weary travellers who have ceased to roam,
Yea, taste the joy divine
Of sons who dwell within their Father's home.

III.

SATURNALIA.

I.

Thick lies the snow upon the Alban height;
The wind sweeps fierce and cold;
And where the summer waters gleaming bright,
Rushed headlong, fold on fold,

Now on the slopes of Tibur hangs the moss,
    All crystal clear with rime,
And spreading elms their vine-clad branches toss
    To greet the winter time.

To Rome they hasten—prætor, poet, sage—
    All but the peasant churl,
And wearied sailors, as the storm-blasts rage,
    Their vessel's white sails furl.

Bronzed legions bring their spoils from furthest East,
    And joy to rest at home ;
From wearied months of toil and march released,
    With quickening step they come.

'Tis time to pile the pine-log on the fire,
    To broach the fragrant cask,
While maid and mother join with son and sire
    To finish all their task.

Then come the days our fathers kept of old,
    When winter snows lay deep,
To great Saturnus in the age of gold,
    Which we will also keep.

And slaves, who toil and moil the whole year round,
    Now for short space are free ;

All hearts are glad, and all good things abound,
    And children shout for glee.

Old jests revive, and ancient songs are sung,
    The peasant's homely mirth ;
Men claim their rights, nor spares the railing tongue
    Pomp, wealth, or pride of birth.

Short gleam of sunshine in the winter cold,
    Bright pause in dreary life ;
Hailed by the young, more welcome to the old,
    Shedding o'er brawls and strife

The freshness and the joy of boyhood's days,
    When skies were bright and clear,
And mirthful voices sang the Gods' high praise,
    Rejoicing year by year.

2.

Come, then, be merry one and all,
Where shines the blaze on hearth and hall,
And household Gods receive the prayer
That floats on incense-cloud through air,
And homage rises, full and strong,
As when, through all the wondering throng,
The victor climbs the heights above,
The hill of Capitolian Jove.

Spare not the sharp and pointed line,
The license of the Fescennine:
The year is ended—let it go;
We cannot check Time's onward flow.
We watched the earliest spring-tide bloom
Start from the dusk of winter's tomb;
We saw the lily and the rose
Unfold their rubies and their snows;
We saw the green corn in the ear
Give promise of the fruitful year,
The golden grain that Ceres gives
As staff of life for all that lives;
And there, where greenest tendrils clasp
The bridegroom elm with bride-like grasp,
And purple clusters hang like gems,
The spoil of Eastern diadems,
We heard the vintage song of joy,
The full-voiced glee of laughing boy,
The home-born drama, rugged rhyme,
True offspring of that golden time.
Then came the huntsman's woodland toil,
The nets, the chase, the savoury spoil,
Laconian hounds, Gætulian spear,
The foaming boar, the dappled deer,
Where groves of oak, and beech, and pine, .
Fling darkness o'er the Apennine.
Then o'er the Adriatic swept
Fierce Auster, and the wild waves leapt;

And Anio, swoln with autumn rains,
Rushed like a torrent on the plains,
And then the days grew short and cold,
The feeble year was waxing old :
At last the death-knell rang, and now,
The fields all bare, and stript each
    bough,
We bid the old, dead year Good-bye,
Watch the red streaks in western sky,
And wait the fresh-born sun that brings
The New Year's blessing on its wings.

Come now, ye lords of high estate,
On worn-out slave and peasant wait,
Let them your goodliest garments don,
The toga, pileus, one by one ;
They sit at table, quaff their wine ;
And ye, the lords of Fabian line,
Who boast the high Cornelian name,
Or share with Gods Iulian fame,
Stand by, quick-eyed each look to catch,
Each want supply, each gesture watch,
As is the boy from Thrace or Gaul,
Who hastens at his master's call.
Ah, lords of men, in senate met,
So like to Gods, that ye forget
Ye share each weak and varying mood
Of all mankind's vast brotherhood,

Now comes your turn for biting jest,
For weary toil that longs for rest :
These slaves and aliens ye despise,
Have sharpest tongues, and keenest eyes ;
That Syrian notes each secret deed,
Your coward sloth, your lust, your greed ;
That Gaul was listening at the door
When ye base words of falsehood swore ;
And now from lips by wine set free
Their flouting jests stream out on thee ;
Thou too art even found as they,
Thy body of the self-same clay.

Rise from your tables, lo! he lifts
That oldest slave, great Saturn's gifts,
The waxen tapers clean and white ;
Come, quickly take them, seize and light ;
From hand to hand the tapers pass,
From man to child, and lad to lass.
Good hope for him whose flame keeps
    clear
Of bright days in the coming year :
Alas ! for him whose feeble hand
Is tardiest in that frolic band,
Who lets the flickering light go out
'Mid looks of triumph, mocking shout ;
Ill omen, or for work or play,
That quenchèd light on Saturn's day.

The quickest foot, the readiest will,
These still their task-work best fulfil,
These labour more and suffer less,
These know the secret of success.
So as the clear flames come and go,
Some rushing quick, some lingering slow,
That taper race of slave and free
A parable of life may be.

3.

And was it nothing more,
That joy and gladness in the heart of man?
The Lord whom we adore,
Hath He not fashioned out life's little span?

Was it then all of earth,
Brute-pleasure of a soul that mates with brutes,
Or did it draw its birth
From Him who gives the seasons and their fruits?

Saturnus, Lord and King,
With whom the old year enters on its rest,—
The offerings that men bring,
Blest in receiving, more in giving blest,—

Oh, tell not these their tale
Of ONE whom men, not knowing Him, adore,

Of ONE who shall not fail,
When harvest, vintage, spring-tide are no more?

This free and open speech
Where man to man speaks out in truest mood,
Does it not wisdom teach,
The gospel of a human brotherhood?

All names and titles gone,
The master and the slave shall one day stand
Before the great white throne,
And there shall gather all from every land.

That race of taper-lights,
Like stars on earth fast flitting through the dark,
Illuming winter nights,
While each to each hands on the glimmering spark,—

Does it not witness bear
Of that great race which all that live must run,
And through each circling year
Press onward, upward, till the goal is won?

We too in darkness move,
Bearing our light amid surrounding gloom,
The light of truth and love,
Still waxing brighter as we near the tomb.

And then when all is o'er,
The light passed on to other hands than ours,
On that eternal shore
Where groves of peace are bright with amaranth flowers,

We, too, as stars shall shine,
No longer in the darkness of the night,
But round the central shrine,
Where dwells the King Eternal in His might ;
And round the throne divine
In order move, a coronal of light.

January 1866.

GILBOA.

I.

SO life is ending, and its visions pass
    Before the inward eye,
Like soft dew falling on the tender grass,
    When all around is dry.

Through the dark night I see the ruby flush
    Of childhood's earliest day ;
Through war's wild din, and battle's torrent rush,
    I hear the children play.

Yet once again I live that time of might,
    When I, and one with me
Who bore my shield, were conquerors in the fight,
    And made the aliens flee.

From crag to crag we clambered, hand in hand,
    And leapt from rock to rock ;
Till from the height we looked on all the land,
    And dared the battle's shock.

I feel the faintness of that noontide heat,
    The thirst that fired the brain;
I taste the golden stream that trickled sweet,
    And brought life back again:

The fear of death is on me as of old,
    When Saul in sternness strove
An iron mantle round his heart to fold,
    And crush a father's love;

I stood as one condemned to shameful death,
    And offered up my life,
As Isaac bowed of old, with calmest breath,
    To meet the glittering knife:

When shrill and loud from warriors old and young
    There rose the awe-struck cry;
Their strong resolve through hill and forest rung,
    "This day shall no man die!"

So with my father many a month passed on,
    I smote the craven foe;
And year by year the crown of victory won,
    Requiting blow for blow:

And robes of scarlet from each plundered town,
    We brought for Israel's maids;
The ruby circlet, and the golden crown,
    Rich harvest of our raids.

So grew my soul to manhood's kingly noon,
    And all men sang my praise ;
Yet darker far than night without a moon,
    Was fame's full daylight blaze.

I craved for one whose heart should beat as mine,
    My hopes and thoughts to share ;
A soul to live with me the life divine,
    And half grief's burden bear.

I sought for one to be my friend and guide,
    My glory and my joy ;
When lo ! there stood in brightness by my side,
    The minstrel shepherd-boy.

II.

Yes, there he stood, and life's deep-hidden fountains
    Welled from my soul in one abounding flood ;
The sun shone brighter on the hoary mountains,
    A sweeter music murmured through the wood.

It was not for the flush of youthful beauty,
    The golden locks that flowed like sunlight down ;
Through eye's wild flash there gleamed the star of
      duty,
    And on his brow Truth set her kingly crown.

Strong arm was his to smite the tyrant stranger,
  Voice soft as maiden's, stirring men to tears,
A soul that knew no fear of death or danger,
  Wide thoughts of wisdom ripening with the years :

Forth from his lips there flowed the song of gladness,
  His hand brought music from the soulless lyre ;
And lo ! the spell chased all the clouds of madness,
  Wrath passed away as wax before the fire.

Of warriors old he sang, our fathers' glory,
  The wonders of the nobler days of old ;
And strong, deep music thrilled through all the story,
  Stirring all hearts to deeds of prowess bold.

He sang the marvels of the earth and heaven,
  The starry night, the cloud-built tent of God,
The wild, dark storm on wings of tempest driven,
  The snow-clad heights where never man has trod :

And new light streamed o'er mountain and o'er river,
  New voices mingled with the streamlet's song ;
Men's hearts rose up to meet the Eternal Giver,
  The slave found freedom, and the weak grew strong.

And oh ! my heart clave to him as he chanted
  The hymns that made the brain and spirit thrill ;
I found the prize for which my soul had panted,
    The friend and guide of thought, and heart, and
      will.

I track that love throughout life's varied chances ;
 And still my heart is with him to the last,
Though all our glory wane as his advances,
 His the bright future, ours the failing past.

III.

'Tis well, 'tis well, I grudge him not the glory,
  His people's love unpriced ;
Long line of kings, great names renowned in story,
  The far-off, coming Christ.

I gave him, in that first bright hour of meeting,
  My robe, and sword, and shield ;
And ofttimes since in every secret greeting,
  In forest or in field,

That sacrifice of self on true love's altar,
  I, of free choice, renewed ;
Nor shall my spirit fail or purpose falter,
  With woman's varying mood.

I trust he loves me still, but love's requiting, . . .
  What need for that to bless ?
Though he should stand a foe against me fighting,
  I should not love him less ;

Though from his hand should dart the spear to slay me,
>   I could not him deny ;
No other love have I whereon to stay me,
>   And when that fails I die :

I dream that he will give a little weeping
>   Above my fameless grave ;
I trust my orphaned child to his true keeping
>   From shame and death to save :

So, though my lineage from the earth shall perish,
>   Yet faithful to the end,
He still, through kingly state and strife, may cherish
>   The memory of his friend.

IV.

That music soft, of tender touch and tone,
That drew the living fount from heart of stone,
>   Is hushed and passed away ;
Now falls the darkness thicker, and mine eye
Looks out upon the starless, moonless sky,
>   The dreary, lonely way.

The king, my father, turned in wild despair
To priest and seer, with unregarded prayer,
>   Seeking for truth and light ;
They answered not, the Urim hid its gleams,
No vision of the future came in dreams,
>   But all was dreariest night ;

And so with frenzy, as of one who feels
The curse of God fall on him while he kneels,
      He in his maddened moods
To Endor turned, where still in cavern drear
Dwelt one, whose name had been a word of fear,
      In sullen solitude.

I shudder yet at what I saw and heard,
The spectral form, the whispered, muttering word,
      The spells that raised the dead,
The low wild chaunt that came like mourner's
    wail,
When o'er the grave sweeps fast the northern gale,
      The lurid light and red,

The kingly face with terror wan and white,
The tall form stretched upon the earth all night,
      The weariness and woe ;
The dreary hours between the midnight black
And day's first gloaming, pale and faint and slack,
      The minutes moving slow ;

The fixed despair, the wild and vacant eye
Of one who hates his life, yet cannot die,
      Though even hope is gone.
Dark end, my father, this of all thy fame,
The songs and shouts that heralded thy name
      The cry of battle won ;

Dark end of all the loftier hours of life
When, raised awhile above its little strife,
   Thy soul rose up to heaven,
And Saul the prophet, bursting into praise,
Sang the great hymns of earlier, holier days,
   Forgiving, and forgiven.

Ah ! even yet I dream there lingers still,
Through wildest storms, and wanderings of the will,
   The man that God will own ;
That loftiest hour thou can'st not all forget,
That glory of the past is with thee yet,
   That music from the Throne.

Yes, he shall own it in whose minstrel notes
A higher strain than priest's or prophet's floats,
   The Spirit from on high ;
His voice shall sing of father and of son,
Who, still unsevered, soul and heart still one,
   In death's dark chamber lie.

Lovely and pleasant yet our names shall be ;
The guilt, the shame, the woe, the pain, shall flee ;
   And, as the shadows fall,
Amid the surging storm, and battle's roar,
We with calm steps approach the eternal shore,
   Where peace reigns over all.

TRANSLATIONS.

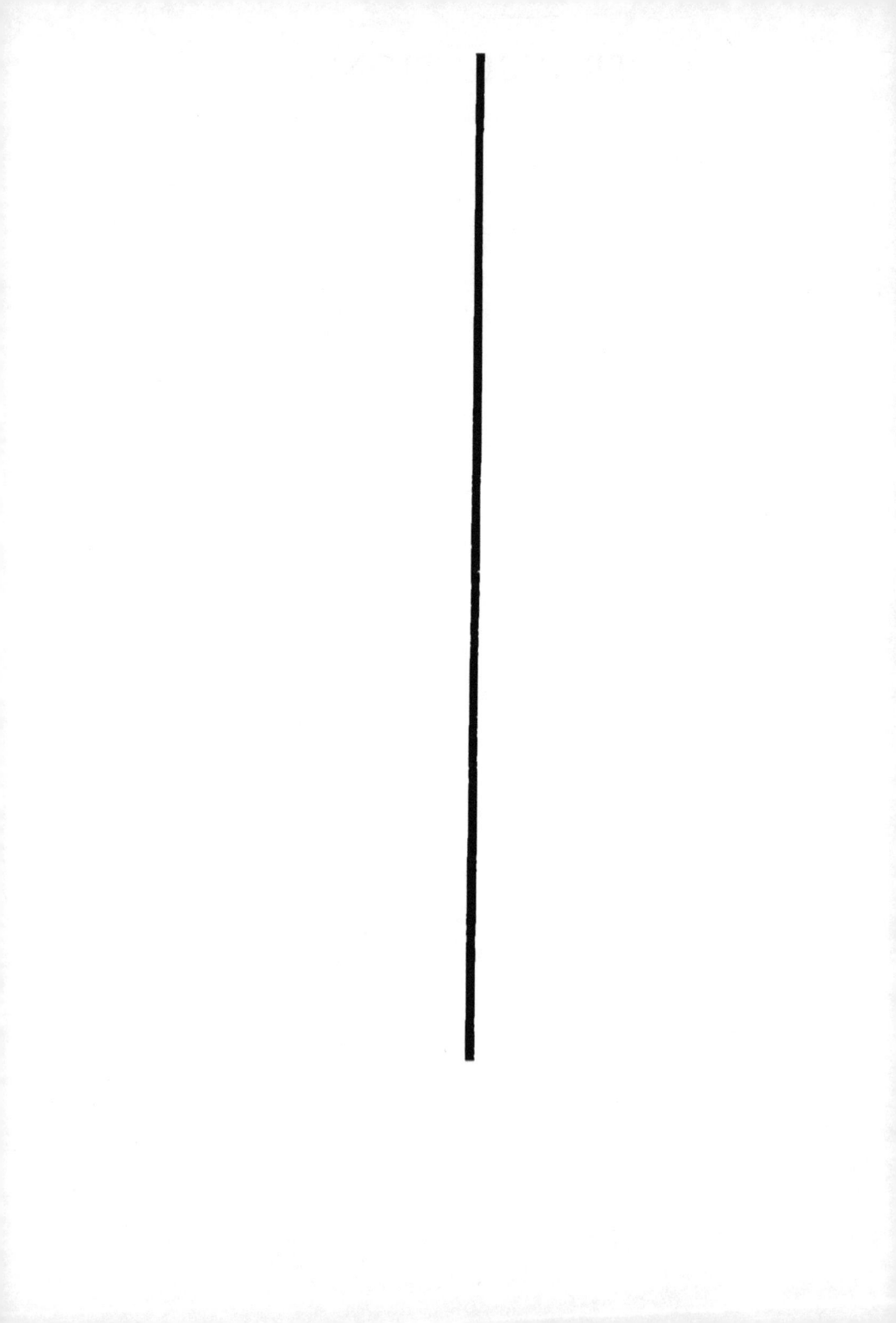

THE SONG OF MOSES AND MIRIAM.

———◆———

I WILL sing to Jehovah, our God; the triumph He
claims as His own :
The horse and his rider lie dead, in the depths of the
waters o'erthrown.
Jehovah my rock and my strength, of Him is my praise
and my song,
From Him our salvation has come, deliverance from falsehood and wrong ;
He, He alone is my God ; my voice shall His majesty
tell ;
The God of my fathers,—to Him shall the floods of our
psalmody swell.
Jehovah has fought on our side, as a warrior mighty to
slay ;
Jehovah, His name, the I AM, through all ages the same
as to-day.

The chariots of Pharaoh are fallen, sunk in the sea wide
and deep ;
And the chief of his riders are with them ; drowned in
the Reed Sea they sleep ;

As a stone sinks, so sank they, for ever. Thy hand, O
    my God, has prevailed ;
Smitten and crushed by Thine arm, the strength of our
    tyrants has failed.
In Thy glory and greatness Thou smotest the people
    against Thee that rose ;
As the fire devoureth the stubble, so went out Thy wrath
    on Thy foes.
At the blast of the breath of Thy nostrils, the waters
    stiffened with fear ;
The waves ceased their ebb and their flow : strange calm
    stayed their course far and near.
Thus in their pride spake our foes, " I will haste, overtake,
    seize the spoil ;
My' hands wield the sword of my vengeance, my soul
    gains the prize of its toil."
With Thy wind Thou did'st blow, and the floods came
    back once again in their might ;
As lead in the mighty waters, they sank in the darkness
    of night.
Who is like Thee, O Jehovah, of all that are mighty and
    strong ?
Dreadful, and holy, and great,—Thy wonders are ever our
    song ;
Thy right hand, stretched forth to destroy, hath smitten
    Thy foes to the grave,
Thy mercy has guided the people Thy power did so won-
    drously save.

In Thy strength Thou hast guided their feet to the land
  that Thou claim'st as Thine own ;
The heathen shall hear it and fear, the Philistines tremble
  and moan ;
The princes of Edom shall cower, smitten with dread and
  dismay ;
Moab's strong ones shall quiver and quail, and Canaan's
  strength melt away.
In their fear and their dread they shall sit, stiffened and
  silent as stone,
Till the people pass over, O Lord, the people Thou claim'st
  as Thine own.
There shalt Thou guide them, and bring to the Mount
  where Thy presence shall shine,
Where, in the place Thou hast chosen, Thy people shall
  kneel at Thy shrine.

The Lord is a King through the ages, eternal the strength
  of His throne :
Come, sing to Jehovah our God; the triumph He claims
  as His own ;
The horse and his rider lie dead, in the depths of the
  waters o'erthrown.

February 1865.

PSALM LXVIII.

I.

Let GOD arise in might,
Let all His foes be scattered far and wide;
Let all be put to flight
Who hate Him in their haughtiness of pride.
As smoke that fleeteth fast,
So drive them, Lord, so drive them on apace;
As wax at furnace-blast,
So let them perish, Lord, before Thy face.
But let the just and good
Rejoice before thee, Lord, for evermore,
Joy in one rushing flood
Of bliss and gladness flowing o'er and o'er.
Yes, sing ye, heart and voice,
Sing praises to the Everlasting Name;
Shout, shout your songs, rejoice
In Him who through the desert rode in flame;
Joyous, with one consent,
Praise the great Name of JAH Omnipotent.

II.

Yes, praise Him, for the Lord our God
Is Father of the fatherless ;
Judge of the lonely widow He,
God in His House of Holiness.
To wanderers in the desert wild '
He gives the joy of tribe and tent,
And brings to freedom's open field
The prisoners chained and bound and spent,
Whilst rebel souls wax faint with thirst,
In howling waste of discontent.

III.

O Lord our God, when Thou of old didst march,
   Before Thy people, through the wilderness,
Earth trembled at Thy presence, and the arch
   Of Heaven was moved Thy glory to confess.

Before Thy might, O God of Israel,
   Proud Sinai quivered at the whirlwind's rage ;
On weary souls the abounding torrents fell,
   And glad streams flowed through all Thine heritage.

The people of Thy chosen ones have found
   A home to dwell in, goodly land and fair
Which Thou, O God, in mercies that abound,
   Dost for Thy people, yea, Thy poor, prepare.

IV.

Jehovah gave the word,
And many a herald maiden spread it wide ;
Great kings fled when they heard,
And Israel's daughters all the spoil divide :

Where, armed in full array,
In pleasant sheepfolds where the calm streams flow,
The hosts their might display,
Like silver dove with wings of golden glow ;

Yea, when the Lord of Might,
Scattered proud kings through all the wide-spread
    field,
Like snow on Zalmon's height,
Gleamed the bright sparkling of the spear and
    shield.

V.

Lofty is Bashan's towering height,
That rears its head, a mount of God,
The topmost peak of all the hills
Is Bashan's summit still untrod.

Why look askance, ye topmost peaks,
That soar all lower heights above,
Against the hill in which He dwells,
The holy place He deigns to love ?

Lo ! twice ten thousand chariots there,
The thousand chariots of our God ;
Jehovah with them rides in state,
Our Sinai is the Lord's abode.

There Thou hast led thy conquered foes,
As captives in captivity ;
To Thee the rebels bring their gifts,
Thou dwell'st among them, Lord most High.

Then bless Jehovah day by day ;
Though men may load our souls with grief,
Yet He will bear our burden still ;
In midst of woe He gives relief.

Jehovah is our God and King,
He still is mighty, strong to save,
And His the upward paths that lead
From out the darkness and the grave.

Yea, God shall smite and lay in dust
The heads of all His haughty foes,
The shaggy locks of all the horde
That proudly dare His might oppose.

VI.

Yea, for the Lord hath said,
I will bring back my people once again ;

Mine own, with ordered tread,
Shall march from Bashan onward to the plain,

As once through depths of sea
They made their way in safety to the shore,
That so they yet may see
Their feet pass on all red with streams of gore ;

That dogs may lick the blood
Which flows, full gushing, from their foemen's veins.
Ah ! then the true, the good
Shall see Thee march victorious through the plains ;

Shall see Thee, Lord and King,
March on in glory to Thy Holy Place.
In front are those that sing,
The minstrels close the rear with measured pace,

And filling all between
The maidens come with timbrel and with song ;
So, where God's flock is seen,
So praise the Lord, ye hosts that march along ;

From Israel's founts of praise
Let the strong flood of Hallelujahs flow :
There Benjamin shall raise,
Weak though he be, his sceptre o'er his foe,

And Judah's chieftains high
Throng thickly round with those Zebulon boasts,
    And chiefs of Naphtali
Shall swell the great procession of our hosts.

    For thee our God hath sent,
O Israel, the strength of His right hand ;
    Work out Thy full intent,
O God, for us, and this our father's land.

    Yea, for Thy temple's sake,
The glory of Jerusalem the blest,
    And so shall princes make
Their offerings of their goodliest and their best,

    Rebuke the beasts that dwell
In reedy thickets on the river's banks,
    Trample on monsters fell,
The fierce young kine that filled the people's ranks,

    Till they their tribute bring ;
Scatter the people eager for the fray ;
    So Mizraim owns her king.
And Cush with clasped hands to our God shall pray.

    Sing therefore to the Lord,
Sing out your songs, all kingdoms of the earth,
    He hath sent forth His word
Throned in high Heaven ere yet the stars had birth,

His voice is strong and loud ;
To Him ascribe the strength of Israel ;
And far above the cloud
His might, and majesty, and glory dwell.

Oh ! wonderful and great
Art Thou, O Lord, in this Thy sanctuary ; '
Thou strength'nest Israel's state ;
Blessed, thrice blessed be our God most high.

August 1865.

THE PRAYER OF CLEMENT OF ALEXANDRIA.

(FROM THE GREEK.)

---◆---

TO Thee, Thou Guide and Friend, I dedicate
    Word-garlands,* which, from meadow yet un-
      touched,
Where Thou hast granted me to roam at will,
My hands have woven, as a working bee
Gathering her harvest from the flowery fields,
Yields from her hive sweet fruit of ceaseless toil,
The comb well-stored with honey, to her lord.
And though I be as one of low estate,
Thy poorest servant, yet 'tis meet to bless
Thy Holy Name from Thine own oracles.
Thou mightiest King of all men, all good things
Bestowing freely, giving noblest gifts,
Father and Lord, Creator of the world,
Who alone mad'st the heavens and all their host,

---

* The "garland" referred to is the treatise of "The Guide," (Pædagogus,) at the conclusion of which this prayer is found.

O

In beauteous order, by thy Word Divine
Adjusting all ; who did'st Thyself appoint
Light, and the day, and to the circling stars
Assign their course unerring, that the sea
And earth might hold their place, and all the round
Of changing seasons orderest in Thy skill,
Winter, spring, summer, and, completing all,
The fruitful autumn ; Thou who did'st create
Out of disorder all this ordered world,
From shapeless matter this fair universe ;—
Grant Thou to me Thy gifts of life, to live
Nobly at all times ; grant Thy grace to me,
Thy Scriptures true to keep in word and deed,
To praise Thee ever, and Thy Word, all-wise,
Of Thee begotten, dwelling still with Thee
Give me, I pray, nor poverty nor wealth,
The simplest store, sufficient for my need,
And chiefly, Father, grant a good man's death.

February 1865.

THE PRAYER OF PRUDENTIUS.*

FATHER in heaven adored,
  Of all creation Lord;
Christ, Co-eternal Son,
And Spirit, Three in One;
Thy wisdom guides my soul,
I bow to Thy control;
And Thou, O Lord, dost give
The breath by which I live;
Before Thy judgment throne
I all my vileness own;
Before that judgment seat
I trust my deeds shall meet
Thy mercy and Thy grace,
Thy smiling, pitying face,
Though what I do or say
Be stained with sin alway.

Before Thee I confess;
Help Thou my wretchedness;
Spare him who owns his sin,
The deep-dyed guilt within:

* The *Peroratio* of the *Hamartigenia.*

I have deserved of Thee
Sin's heaviest penalty ;
But Thou, O Judge, be kind,
Cast all deserts behind ;
Hear, Lord, the prayer of woe,
And better things bestow.

Grant this poor soul of mine,
When it shall leave its shrine
Of flesh, skin, blood, and bone,
The house it calls its own,
To which it fondly clings,
In love of earthly things ;
When death's sad hour shall close
These eyes in dark repose,
And worn and spent shall lie
This frail mortality :
When, cleansed and clear, the
        sight
Shall see the soul's true light :
Oh, hide Thou then from view,
The fierce, wild robber crew,
That fright the startled ear
With voice and look of fear,
Who fain would drag me down,
Sin-stained from foot to crown,
To caverns drear and deep,
And there a prisoner keep

Till all I owe be paid,
Guilt's utmost farthing weighed.

Within Thy Father's home
In different order come,
O Christ, the mansions meet,
Each soul's assigned retreat:
I ask not with the blest
To gain eternal rest;
There let the saints abide
Who conquered lust and pride,
And, seeking riches true,
From earth's vain shows withdrew.
There, in perpetual youth
Let white-souled, maiden Truth,
For ever dwell on high,
In stainless chastity:
For me, for me 'tis well,
If no dread form of Hell,
No face that fills with fear,
Shall meet my spirit there;
If only Thou restrain
Gehenna's fire and pain,
Nor leave my soul to flit
All hopeless to the pit:
Enough, if fleshly stain
Require the cleansing pain,

That in the lake of fire
I purge each foul desire :
Only let breezes sweet
Temper the slackening heat,
And scorching flames abate
The fierceness of their hate.
The boundless realm of light,
The crown of glory bright,—
This meed let others gain ;
Enough, if I attain,
Beneath Thy pitying eye,
A lighter penalty.

March 1865.

DJELADEDDIN'S CONFESSION.

(FROM THE PERSIAN.*)

———◆———

THOU only source of life and wisdom true,
   O Lord our God! we sin exceedingly;
Who on life's journey dost our souls renew;
O Lord our God! we sin exceedingly.

Thou only Lord, Thy hands thou openest wide;
Mighty art Thou, and none is good beside;
Thy mercy flows in one abounding tide;
O Lord our God! we sin exceedingly.

Our earthly lusts have wrapt us round with chains,
Our poor, low wishes bring the bond-slave's pains,
We search all madly for forbidden gains;
O Lord our God! we sin exceedingly.

All weak and poor are we, and full of shame,
Through a far land we wander, blind and lame,
Our body's burden marks us heirs of blame;
O Lord our God! we sin exceedingly.

* This, and the two following poems, are translated from *Von Rosenzweig's* German version.

Those that bow low at Heaven's eternal door,
We hear them sing Thy praises evermore,
In speech or silence still Thy name adore;
O Lord our God! we sin exceedingly.

Before Thy face all evil melts away,
All sins Thou pardonest in Thy mercy's day,
Thy grace and love Thou grantest us alway;
O Lord our God! we sin exceedingly.

Now tangled round with earth's vain visions bright,
Now rapt in ecstasy to endless light,
The great Workmaster still left out of sight;
O Lord our God! we sin exceedingly.

Like nightingale's sad song at break of day,
Our wailing voice breathes forth its plaint alway,
And, full of grief and longing, still we say,
O Lord our God! we sin exceedingly.

Thou King! whose wisdom knows to loose or bind,
Behold Thy servants, weak, and poor, and blind,
Who in Thy love alone their refuge find;
O Lord our God! we sin exceedingly.

Thou veilest o'er Thy servants' countless sins,
From Thee our soul its grace and glory wins.

Thy mighty word will end what it begins ;
O Lord our God ! we sin exceedingly.

O leave us not to perish evermore
In sins, which we with weeping eyes deplore,
Though still they swell the dread, accusing score ;
O Lord our God ! we sin exceedingly.

Hear, Lord !　All night I cry in strong desire,
My love for Thee is in my heart as fire,
I fain would join th' exulting seraph-choir ;
O Lord our God ! we sin exceedingly.

February 1865.

ONWARD.

(FROM DJELADEDDIN RUMI.)

———◆———

THE form thou see'st in beauty's glowing ray
    Hath its beginning in the things that die;
Yet though it change, the archetype shall stay:
    Burst then the fetters, cease to mourn and sigh:
The mirrored glory that has given thee gladness,
    The sweet discourse, as music to thine ear,—
O! when they vanish, sit not down in sadness,
    Thou may'st not look for lasting rapture here.

If yon true, primal spring must ever flow,
    The little fountain shall not shrink and dry;
If both are full, nor change and failure know,
    Why falls the tear, why comes the frequent sigh?
'Tis thine, the fountain in thy soul beholding,
    In things of earth the streamlets still to see;
'Tis thine to trust that fount of joys unfolding,
    Whence the small streams, unbidden, flow to thee.

From that first moment, full of issues vast,
　　When thou did'st enter this world's narrowing clime,
Through all the change of present and of past
　　Thou find'st a ladder set for thee to climb.
Lifeless at first, thou had'st thy birth's beginning,
　　Then came the life thou share'st with plants and trees ;
Then one step onward, higher brute-life winning :
　　Hast thou not eyes to look on things like these ?

Soon came the man, expanding in thy soul,
　　Who to his faith adds wisdom's golden lore ;
And then thy body's growth made up the whole,
　　Which yet is nought but dust from earth's poor store ;
And when as man the appointed time thou spendest,
　　An angel shalt thou be in yon blest choirs ;
And, heir of bliss, when this life's course thou endest,
　　In Heaven's high home find all thy heart's desires.

Nor even then shall angels' joy be all ;
　　But thou shalt plunge all boldly in the deep,
And thy poor drop shall in the ocean fall,
　　Wherein a thousand seas of rapture sleep.
Wherefore, my son, refrain from all thy striving,
　　And from thy true heart speak in tones of joy,
" The soul still waxes strong, its youth reviving,
　　Though the poor body faint with earth's annoy."

February 1865.

MORNING COUNSEL.

(FROM DJELADEDDIN RUMI.)

———◆———

A WAKE, my soul, thy homage pay,
    For prayer and praise are noblest deed;
Pure joy is his, and his alone,
    Whose soul from sleep's dull chain is freed.
If thou, my friend, wilt strengthen faith,
    Wake up when morning's dawn is gray;
Wake up, and so attain the prize,
    The Eden bliss of endless day.
" Up, sluggard, up ! the East is clear,"
    So sounds the cock's shrill clarion call ;
Yet thou, all drunk with sleep, know'st not
    The joys that to the wakeful fall.
Thy faint heart says, " I rise, I rise,"
    Thy senses whisper, " Wait awhile :"
Curb, then, thy sense ; for, lo ! the days
    Ensnare thy soul with subtlest guile.
Thou poor, weak, helpless heir of flesh,
    Thou slave of lust, and sloth, and pride,

Bethink thee still, from day to day,
   Death standeth ever by thy side.
'Tis well, lift up thine heart on high,
   While still thine eyes weep pearly tears ;
Escape from folly's vain deceit,
   Of all thy foes the fear of fears.
Though thou wert Sultan of Tebriz,
   And bright as morn when shadows flee,
Yet thou in dust shalt one day lie,
   And pride's fond dreams are not for thee.

February 1865.

THE CRIES OF ISRAEL.

I.—THE TENTH CENTURY.*

WEARY and long are the years,
  Sorrow grows more and more ;
Scarcely we rest from our fears,
  Our trouble never is o'er.
All the seasons pass on,
  No sign is seen in the sky ;
Each ends as each has begun,
  The ages darkly glide by ;
And the grief is harder to bear,
  Old sorrow in newest array.
I dreamt that Redemption was near,
  I saw the dawn of its day ;
Yet still the troubles remain,
  Still, though they swore it would come ;
And they fix new seasons again,
  And they tell us of glory and home.

* Rabbi Joseph : Zunz. *Synagogal Poesie* p. 213.

So the days of the exile glide on,
  In dreams, delusion, and woe,
" To-day or to-morrow the sun
  Will gladden all hearts with its glow ;"
And the faithful count up the days,
  Tell out their tale, and are glad ;
But none of us knoweth Thy ways ;
  Vain yearning maketh us sad.

2.—THE FIRST CRUSADE—MAYENCE.*

Yes, they slay us and they smite,
Vex our souls with sore affright ;
All the closer cleave we, Lord,
To Thine everlasting word.
Not a word of all their Mass
Shall our lips in homage pass ;
Though they curse, and bind, and kill,
The living God is with us still.
Yes, they fain would make us now,
Baptized, at Baal's altars bow ;
On their raiment, wrought with gold,
See the sign we hateful hold ;
And, with words of foulest shame,
They outrage, Lord, the holiest Name :

* Kalonymos ben Jehuda : Zunz. *Synagogal Poesie,* p. 16.

We still are Thine, though limbs are torn ;
Better death than life forsworn.
Noblest matrons seek for death,
Rob their children of their breath ;
Fathers, in their fiery zeal,
Slay their sons with murderous steel,
And in heat of holiest strife,
For love of Thee, spare not their life.
The fair and young lie down to die
In witness of Thy Unity ;
From dying lips the accents swell,
"Thy God is One, O Israel ;"
And bridegroom answers unto bride,
"The Lord is God, and none beside ;"
And, knit with bonds of holiest faith,
They pass to endless life through death.

August 1865.

ST THERESA.

(FROM MAURICE DE GUERIN.)

———◆———

THERESA, holy maid, of Jesus loved,
    Bride of the Lord, a pure dove consecrate,
At last I have thy likeness.   From the day
When first I knew thy story wonderful,
When first I read those lines of thine, where love,
Thy love supreme, has all unconsciously
Wrought out Heaven's own true poem, I resolved
To have one as mine own, or old or new,
A picture with thy name.   And Heaven has willed
At last that I should find the graven print,
Such as I wished, impression clear and good,
And in design not all unworthy thee :
Were it less perfect, still above all else
My love 'twould gain.   Thy name is grace enough ;
And thus, my saint, thy form is painted there :

The scene a church : well chosen ! that in truth
Was thine asylum, fondly cherished.   There

P

Thou bendest one knee only on the stone,
The other half inclines, and robe of serge,
Low falling down, with no ingathered folds,
Leaves one fair foot divinely peeping forth ;
That gracious foot, which just a sandal bears,
Spotless and white as snow, is on the flag ;
And thou dost bend a little, as though limbs
Were weary, at a column's foot, one arm
Upon its elbow, resting on the base ;
And thy two hands, each in the other clasped,
Like two fair sisters, meet in sweet embrace.
A linen fold upon thy brow serene
Like a clear light marks out the gracious line,
And from that brow so pure there shines and falls,
Like white cloud glittering on a stainless dawn,
A band, the Sister's token, to the neck,
And, with its whiteness, whiteness hides from view.
A linen mantle falling to the ground
Rolls its light texture into airy folds,
And on the head a veil well thrown behind,
Forms screen of leafage for our summer rose,
While in the air, just floating near the brow,
Shines a clear circlet of a silver light,
The airy crown in lines of finest touch,
With which the heads of all the saints are crowned.
And was that all ?   I had forgot the cross
Which serves for prayer, and at thy girdle hangs,
Ending thy rosary.   Nor should I fail

To note, thus speaking of the cross, that there
In all the Church it stands the only one.
Nor other altar is there.   Thy pure form
Is living in its grace of holiest thought;
It is a joy to pass a whole day's length
Before that form, and stir not; it is joy
To give thee all my love.   But painter's skill,
Wanting in faith, has given no heed to this,
That thou should'st look on Him who looks on thee,
That Christians when they pray bend low their eyes,
That eyes full open scarce can pray aright.

Here in the chamber where I live, poor cell,
Theresa, thou hast been companion true
Of a poor soul, ill-handled of the world,
Who in his heavenward path drags weary foot.
There thou dost hang, dear picture, best beloved
In frame where yet the faded gilding shines,
On the carved woodwork that surmounts my couch,
My saint by day, my vision all the night;
And just below the white *benitier* hangs,
And in its shell some drops of water holds,
Such as foul spirits shun, and, night by night,
I come to dip my finger's tip therein;
Or were it better said that prayer drinks there.
Winging its flight to yonder heavenly clime,
As I have seen the birds of travel do?
I know not, but I feel when hot and worn

My brow has borne throughout the day some dream
Too lofty, when I have allowed chance thoughts
To settle there, and leave their burning trace,
I feel, I say, at evening, when my hand,
Dipped in this water, touches it, that ill
Is turned to good.

      Theresa, whom I love,
Queen of my cell, thou see'st full oft my brow
Burns hot, and I, poor sinner, am constrained
To turn mine eyes from thee in very fear
Lest thy fair angel-look with blush of shame
O'erspread my cheek, for often through my soul
Something will pass which makes the outspread hands
· Too little to conceal the guilty face.
When eyes serene, clear sky, the loveliness
Of universal nature, yea, a dove,
A simple dove, in snow-white plumage clad,
All this torments us, and we seem to shrink
From purest whiteness of fair innocence ;—
Ah, when from thee I shrink, dear virgin mine,
I pray thee, look not on my sin-stained soul ;
Let not our glances meet. I only ask
This compromise between us. Glances none ;
That stands agreed. When evil chance shall come,
Thou wilt have pity on me ; I in turn
Will trust in thee, and that *benitier* white,
Which hangs near thee shall as the channel serve
By which to hold communion. Thou shalt leave,

As 'twere an alms, a little water-drop
To heal mine ills, such water as men give
To fainting souls, and I, poor beggar found,
Weary and worn, in it will take that alms.

January 1865